THE MISTRESS

A PARANORMAL PREGNANCY ROMANCE

JASMINE WHITE

Get Yourself a FREE Bestselling Paranormal Romance Book!

Join the "**Simply Shifters**" Mailing list today and gain access to an exclusive **FREE** classic Paranormal Shifter Romance book by one of our bestselling authors along with many others more to come. You will also be kept up to date on the best book deals in the future on the hottest new Paranormal Romances. We are the HOME of Paranormal Romance after all!

* Get FREE Shifter Romance Books For Your Kindle & Other Cool giveaways

* Discover Exclusive Deals & Discounts Before Anyone Else!

* Be The FIRST To Know about Hot New Releases From Your Favorite Authors

Click The Link Below To Access Get All This Now!

SimplyShifters.com

Already subscribed?
OK, *Turn The Page!*

About This Book

She never meant to become his mistress, it just sort of happened. Now Tara Newhart is going to have pay a price for her actions. A very **BIG** price.

After joining a secret wolf pack, Tara never felt so alone. She knew no one and no one seemed to want to make her feel welcome.

No one apart from the Alpha Grayson Wilkes, that is.

Having been given an arranged mate, Grayson has never truly loved his mate and after meeting Tara he felt he had finally met a woman he could genuinely love.

However, the punishment for infidelity within the pack is death.

This is quite some risk, but it is a risk both Grayson and Tara feel is worth taking..

CHAPTER ONE

New York City was the kind of place that there was no real difference between falling asleep and waking up.

It was the kind of world where everyone just sort of turns continually and you were the one who changed. In fact, the more you thought about New York, the more it seemed to be alive and living a life that was actually a lot better than her own. It was something that she came to realize when she moved to this city. Brooklyn wasn't the place that she thought it would be when she was first living in the city, but she quickly realized that it was more than just a collection of buildings. It was a living, breathing thing just as much as she was. But, in the end it was just her living in this enormous, sprawling creature.

Opening her eyes to the alarm going off next to her bed, Tara looked out the window and saw the frozen, dreary world of soon-to-be January. It was the kind of world that lost all the magic that winter was given by the gift of Christmas. Take away Christmas and all you had was a miserable, desolate cold that seemed to last forever. It was the long, hard push to spring and right now, Tara felt a little depressed. It was New Year's Eve and this was truly the last day that they were going to have the opportunity to enjoy anything out of January. She felt her heart sag as she looked at the flurries drifting through the air and she knew that she was going to regret going outside.

But, it was one of the days where she was going to make more than ever on tips and it was going to give her a good haul. Working at a club wasn't an ideal job, but when she came to the city, she had nothing. She was a Shifter far from home, looking for a pack to call her own. They had accepted her into the pack with nothing but open arms and smiles. Of course, when she looked around her apartment, thought of her job, and thought about how those smiles had faded over the passing year, she felt nothing but a hollow sadness inside of her.

In Minnesota, Tara had been something of a big deal. She'd been one of the prettiest girls in all of Rookwood and the envy of every man that she bumped into. Sure, she'd been cocky and she'd been a bit of a tease, but when the hunters came for her family and she was forced to go on the run, things changed for her.

She didn't know what happened to her parents, but the fact that they never came to find her told her more than she ever needed to know. So here in New York City, she was forced to start over and when she met the Wilkes Pack, she was excited just to have found other wolf Shifters just like herself, but the feeling of jubilee and excitement faded quickly.

None of the women who had been in the pack for longer than she had liked the idea of a hot, sexy young woman coming in and drawing the attention of the males. Sure, they all looked human enough, but the animalistic urges and the primal lust that was inside of all of them was something that had to be addressed. The women of any Shifter pack or tribe were fiercely territorial. So, Tara was thrown down the rabbit's hole and left to serve as the lowest part of the pack.

But, it wasn't without its perks. She had a home to live in, a pack that would protect her from other Shifters or hunters. She had a job where her attractive little self would be put to good use, drawing in customers and making them tip more than they would for anyone else. When she thought about it, she would get depressed by the fact that there were children more important in the pack than her. But she would rise. It would take time, but one day, she was going to find a mate and she was going to be just fine.

Walking into the bathroom, Tara turned on the shower and brushed her teeth as she thought about the insanity and the chaos that was going to unfold that day. It was going to be one of those days where she was extremely grateful that she had the job that she had.

She took off her tank top and her pants, slipping her panties off as she stepped into the shower and felt the warmth flood across her skin, filling her up with excitement and encouragement. There in the early morning hours, the only thing she had to get excited about was her shower. It was enough to make her want to actually get ready. She felt the weight of the night and yesterday wash off her as she shampooed her hair and rinsed the soap off her body.

Feeling ready for the day, she stepped out of the shower and dried herself off and then finished with her short brown hair, looking at how frizzy it was. There was a number of different things that she had to do throughout her whole process of getting ready. She would always start with makeup and that would usually take around half an hour for her to get done on a daily basis. She always did her hair last.

Tara learned when she was younger that makeup was one of those things that couldn't really make you more beautiful, it just gave off the illusion of that. What it did do was give her extra confidence to go out in the world and not be afraid of who she was. As far as she was concerned, all those people who told her that she was the most beautiful woman that they'd ever seen were liars.

There was no one in the world as unimpressed by Tara's beauty as she was. She was completely disappointed in herself, but there were very few people who shared that sentiment. When she looked in the mirror, she would see glimmers of that truth, but she locked it out and she kept it hidden away from her.

Finishing up with her makeup, she quickly realized she had to get dressed and there was only one uniform for her to wear. When you work at the Gilded Globe, there was nothing for you to do but wear gold and white. It was something that made the women distinguished and different from all the other clubs in the world, let alone the entire city. It was quite the accomplishment, but honestly, it was nothing but a front for Shifters and packs to meet and conduct business on a slightly neutral territory.

High white boots, a white short skirt with gold embellishments, and a white top that was adorned with as much gold as possible. When she looked at herself, she couldn't help but feel like there was something about her that made her feel like she was in a music video or something close to that. It wasn't the most glorifying job and it wasn't the most impressive, but there was a benefit to it.

She looked good in it and there was no forgetting that. Everything about it made her tantalizing and an object of affection for anyone who was interested in her. She smiled and stood up, looking at her reflection as she grabbed her long, white coat and headed for the door. She was already exhausted, but that still meant that there was a whole day of exhaustion ahead of her. She wasn't excited about that, but this was what was waiting for her.

Days were getting longer and they were getting more exhausting with each passing day. One day, she knew that there was going to be a break, but as she headed downstairs, she looked at herself in the mirror again, her long legs clad in white leather, her ass perky and her body fit for whatever was waiting for her the rest of the day. Looking at the woman in the mirror, she knew that she was a force to be reckoned with, but she couldn't help but feel sad and lonely.

The pack didn't seem interested in her or with the idea of letting her advance along in the ranks. They were more interested in keeping the status quo. At first, she had just been grateful, but now it was beginning to feel like a prison sentence. She knew that they would just keep her around as a carrot to throw at some male that they wanted joining the pack or that they wanted to pull away from some other group.

She was a token gift to be handed out, a prize for deciding that their pack was worth coming to. Already, she could feel the elders trying to figure out what it was that they were going to get out of Tara's presence in the pack.

There was only one person who was actually interested in seeing her as a member of this pack and the one person that she was most terrified of having any kind of curiosity about. Grayson Wilkes was the second most powerful man in the entire pack and he was the man being groomed to take the place of his father the moment he passed. He would be the head of the pack, the Alpha.

He would be in charge of one of the most powerful packs in all of New York City and in all of the world. Essentially, he would be in the process of becoming a king to his own little kingdom. Of course, there was a lot that he would have to negotiate and handle the responsibility of, but he would be more powerful than most power-hungry men could dream of. His eyes were wide with hunger and the one thing that he was most ravenous for now was the affections of Tara.

The only problem with that was the fact that he was already promised to another and that other woman was fiercely territorial and fiercely protective of the man that she was married to. They were mates, or so it was declared, since they were children. It was the making of a marriage that added an extra forty people to the pack that was already substantially large, but gluttonous for more.

Harriet Wilson was the woman who brought the pack the numbers that made it the most powerful pack in the whole city. But, while she lived in an upscale penthouse in Manhattan, Tara was at the bottom of the pack, slumming it in Brooklyn that was barely better than living in a shoebox.

It had crossed her mind that the only reason that Grayson ever showed her an ounce of interest was the fact that she was politically powerless to refuse him if she ever wanted to and that he would have the kind of deniability that would be ironclad to his cause. No one would believe that he was picking from the dregs of the pack, even if Tara was the most attractive Shifter in the pack.

No one would buy it. But that was the kind of cynical thinking that Tara tried her hardest to avoid and some that she knew was nothing more than a lie that her mind had conjured up to scare her and make her feel weak and pathetic. No, there was much more to this than just the fact that she was pretty and he was looking for some attention where he wasn't getting it at home.

There were multiple sources that whispered that Harriet wasn't the kind of lover that any man would want and from what Tara knew about Grayson, he was far too kind to even try to broach the subject with her. He wasn't the kind of man to approach conflict unless it was absolutely necessary. He wasn't the warrior and the gangster that his father had been. No, he was a kinder soul who believed in negotiations, diplomacy, and good will toward one another.

He wasn't the kind of person that you'd want in a fight, but he was the kind that you'd want to be at the head of the group, keeping you out of a fight. She liked him. She liked his personality and he was easily the most handsome person that she'd ever seen. That was what was making it more difficult.

With the amount of troubles that mounted for Shifters, it was a surprise that there wasn't more of a demand for a man like Grayson to be in charge. He was the man who was going to make sure that they were alive and safe, after all was said and done. Between rival packs and hunters roaming around every corner, someone who knew how to negotiate was going to be the single most valuable asset that a leader could have.

 Right now, Hugh Wilkes was a man of action and danger, not of understanding and compromise. Hopefully, Grayson was going to change all of that. He was going to be the man that took care of them.

Taking a deep breath, she wrapped her scarf around her neck and stepped out into the frigid, dying days of December, looking for a cab. It was going to make everything feel worse today. No one liked the cold and she hated it more than most. When the taxicab pulled over for her, she hopped in and she headed straight for the Gilded Globe. She was the kind of person who didn't mind taking a cab even in the age of uber domination.

The Gilded Globe was gaudy and there was no hiding from it. As she looked at the exterior with its white columns, adorned in gold and with ornate, art deco windows, she couldn't help but wonder how much money they funneled into this place when they were building it. Inside was a mixture of faux black marble tiles, crown molding, enormous mirrors, chandeliers, and everything was either black, gold, crystal, or white.

The whole place was bathed in faux elegance. It was the kind of elegance that made her feel like a charlatan, but it made those who came to visit the club feel like they were a higher class of customer. With beautiful women roaming around in tight clothing and handsome men behind the bar, that did the trick for them.

It was the kind of foolish that people actually fell into this little obvious trick that the club pulled on them, but there was nothing to it. Every club and every restaurant with attractive women all pulled the same trick. It drew the men in and they liked to tip for it. Whenever Tara walked home with a large tip, she always felt better about it. Besides, there was plenty of people who hit on her and belittled her when it came to her being a waitress. They would slap her ass or they would try and feel her up when she was working. So in the end, she didn't feel that bad about the kind of haul that she would make on average.

When you walked into the Gilded Globe, there was something about the place that made you feel special. It was an entry that allowed people to check their coats and bags if they needed to, but more importantly it filled people with excitement. The white and gold statues reached up and held up the vaulted ceiling, swelling the world with a sense of wonder and duty.

She looked at everything around her and felt like she was given the opportunity to stay in a palace, enjoying everything that was offered there. She walked past the entryway, smiling at Billy who worked the coat check and made sure that everyone was working correctly and paying attention to what their jobs were.

There was one thing that their boss hated more than anything, it was the inefficiency of employees who don't follow orders properly. Sure, they might be beautiful and they might get a lot of business for the Gilded Globe, but they were always expendable. There were plenty of people who were eager to take their place if they couldn't perform properly.

"Hey Tara," Billy called cheerfully. He had a crush on her, but it wasn't unique. It wasn't the kind of thing that lasted long. In fact, there were plenty of people for him to have a crush on. Honestly, Tara didn't hold it as anything more than a passing fancy, because at the rate her love life was going, there was no hope in people actually sticking around for long.

The main room of the Gilded Globe was something that was more than magnificent. It was the very definition of opulence and it had all the elegant beauty that the entry way had, but more. It was dark, lit only by the chandeliers that filled the room with as much light as it needed, reflecting and dancing off of the glossy and gilded surfaces all around the room.

As she looked at the room, it always impressed her. It had been so many weeks of coming to this place and punching in and then punching out, but while the daily grind got repetitive, this place never failed to impress her.

The view was everything and when she looked at the bar and the white marble counter with golden lights, she knew that this was the place that made people feel like they were gods and that was all that mattered to most people. That was what they wanted out of their life. They wanted to come here, kick back, and feel like they were going to be the heroes of their own story.

This was their manufactured paradise.

She looked at her friends who were working in the room. Tina and Laura were already there, sitting around the large banquet table on the second tier. They looked over at her and waved, grinning as she crossed the room with all the poise and elegance that she had learned while being employed at the club. If you wanted to impress people here, you needed to be able to work with what you had. Just having resources at your disposal wasn't enough, you had to know how to showcase your beauty, how to give the world what it wanted. That was the task that she had set herself to since she started working at the Gilded Globe.

The main room was divided up into two areas. There was tier one, which consisted of the dance floor, the entryway, and the bar. All of these were usually where there were the kind of people that she liked to avoid while she was at work. This was where they danced, mingled, tested each other out, and taught their partner how to grind. This was where drunken fools got handsy and the bouncers were supposed to rein them in. If there was ever a problem, sixty percent of the time, it was on tier one. That was because drunken people liked to brawl and fight over girls on the dance floor. Even if the confrontation started on tier two, it always ended up blowing up on the dance floor. Girls always tried the same tactic when their man was getting angry with a suitor. They would always whisper, "Let's go dance!" in their ear, practically shouting it.

That was when the suitor, or the jealous ex, or the crashing and burning boyfriend followed their object of affection and desire out onto the dance floor. After that, was when the shoving and the pushing started. Then the bouncers would swoop in from tier two, Tara and the other serving girls would shake their heads in disappointment.

Tier two was where Tara and the other serving girls worked. It had access to the kitchen and it had access to the DJ booth. Down four stairs and you were at the bar or the dance floor, but Tara and the other girls never actually went to the dance floor. As far as she was concerned, that was No Man's Land. She looked at it as a minefield that would kill her if she dared to go out there.

Tier two wrapped around the dance floor and hugged the wall, lined with booths and small tables for people who liked to cluster around a plate of overpriced food or drinks. It was a kind of docking bay for girls who wanted one place to load up their purses and hold them tight before they hit the dance floor. The large banquet table was usually reserved for special events or really large parties that all wanted to stick together, but honestly, it was usually utilized most by having these staff meetings.

Above them was the mezzanine, which had more seating, usually for meetings or people who were looking for more of a date experience. It was a cozy and a comfortable area with intimate seating, soft lighting, and furniture that was more comfortable than tier two. When you sat on the mezzanine, you had the opportunity to spend the evening with the person that you cared about most and to show them what it was to be a special person in the world.

All of it looked down on the dance floor and gave you access to it if you wanted to, but Tara rarely saw anyone on the mezzanine ever descend to the dance floor. These were classy people looking for a classy night with whoever had struck their attention.

The last part of the Gilded Globe was the other side of the second story where the VIP club was off limits. It was the kind of place where Shifters usually made back room deals and where very famous people would visit when they stopped by the Gilded Globe. They were the kind of people who liked the privacy and they enjoyed the personal bar in the VIP room and the servers who were discreet and were professional, not gushing over them or making a big deal about their presence.

Tara worked the VIP room on certain nights, but she hated it. People who were in the VIP room had to call and make reservations and they were usually nobodies who had a lot of money to throw around and look like they were a big deal. They liked it when people saw how much money they made in whatever job in financing, marketing, or managing that they had. They were a bunch of bureaucratic punks who were blazing now, but would be gone tomorrow. It was easy to pretend like they were no different than the customers across the floor at the mezzanine. She had very little respect for anyone who occupied the VIP room.

All in all, her job was about making people feel good. Her job was to make sure that patrons thought that she saw them as special and that she found them very important. They wanted to think that when they had Tara's attention, they were the only people in the world that mattered. Though it was as far from the truth as it possibly could be, she knew that there was something off about all of it.

It rang hollow inside of her lately and it was something that just made her feel like she was a prostitute, paid to make people feel good, but they couldn't touch. It was like being an escort. It made her feel empty inside, because no one wanted to take care of her.

No one wanted to know what it was like in Tara's world. They just wanted to take from her and they wanted to fantasize about what it was like to be her and that was the end of it. None of them were interested in actually seeing what it was like to have her in their life.

As she plopped down in the seat next to Tina, she knew that she was just feeling sorry for herself and she was pitying herself. There was nothing to it. She didn't need to feel like she was worthless, she just needed to have a real relationship. For the past four months, she had been courted and romanced by a man who pretended like she was nothing and when she was with him, she was captivated by him.

She was caught up in his presence and there was nothing that she wanted more than to give him everything that he could ever want from her, but at times like now, she felt hollow and empty. He couldn't ever have her for himself and she could never call him her man.

She knew that she was going to be alone forever, playing the role of the mistress to the man who never wanted to get married in the first place to his wife. It was a sad and depressing place to be and she knew that there was something wrong with her.

She needed to get a real relationship. She needed to find someone who was going to care about her and do anything for her. She needed a man who would throw himself into danger, because he loved her that much. It was something that she longed for and she knew if a guy slapped her on the ass, there was nothing that Grayson could do to him.

There was nothing that he could possibly do that would show his care for her. She was nothing to him. She had to be nothing to him. That was the most painful part of all of it. She took a deep breath and smiled, knowing that it wouldn't be long now.

People were flooding into the Gilded Globe and they were taking their places around the enormous black table that was adorned with gold and silver, intricately made and crafted. It was a gorgeous table, but everyone was sitting somewhere that was designated by their group's area.

The bouncers were in one area, valet and entryway in another, the kitchen staff by themselves, the bartenders between the valets and the final group, the serving staff. It was the kind of division that became cliquish really quickly, but they were all friends here and they all knew that no matter what, at the end of the day, they were all Gilded Globe employees and family. They had each other's back.

The saddest part was that the Gilded Globe felt more like a family to Tara than her actual pack. They were supposed to be her family, but there were only three other pack mates here and the rest were humans, unaware that they were mingling with the mythical. Tina, Laura, and Greg were the only people here who were Shifters with her and they had a special bond because of that. Of course, Luke, their manager, was also a Shifter, but she didn't really count him. He was so beyond her realm of friendship that it wasn't worth even noting him. Besides, she only saw her on days like this.

"Won't be long now," Laura let out a sigh.

"Until what?" Tara asked.

"Didn't you hear?" Laura sounded genuinely surprised. When she saw the look on Tara's face, she laughed and shook her head. "The Prince himself is coming down here to greet us. Apparently there's some big deal happening up in the VIP room tonight and he's going to be making sure that this place is spotless and in tip-top shape himself."

"Grayson's coming here?" Tara asked, feeling her soul breathe a sigh of relief, but it was quickly encapsulated by the terror of what that meant.

Grayson was coming here.

CHAPTER TWO

When you worked at the Gilded Globe, you became a part of a very tense, very high strung family that operated efficiently and accepted absolutely no weakness. If you slowed down the train, then you were quickly thrown off. Those who got their job at the Gilded Globe, tended to look up at the golden sphere hanging above the dance floor and think that they had made it to the big leagues of entertainment.

The truth was, they were just on probation and if they didn't fit in, didn't do their job right, or just sucked at anything, they were kicked out faster than they could sneeze. But, if you made it through your first five shifts without pissing anyone off or without majorly screwing up, the job was yours and you were officially part of the strangest family in the world.

It wasn't long until you started to figure out where your place was in the world, because once you stepped through those towering black and gold doors, you were in the Globe's universe and that meant that you were officially a slave working for the almighty dollar that lined the manager's pocket.

But, there was freedom in knowing what it was that you were supposed to do, who your team was, and just where it was that you fit in. Sure, people shuffled around and rose up the ranks, some people moved away or moved on, but most just stuck around and kept getting better and better at their tiny little tasks until they were perfect in every way.

It wasn't long until Tara realized where she fit in the spectrum of the Gilded Globe's family and what it meant for her to be a part of her particular family. She was teamed up with Tina and she had helped bring up Laura and the three of them were now the closest friends in the entire room. They reached out to make Greg a part of their group, making them the quartet, but Greg was kind of a shadow operative of their friendship.

They would hang out together off the clock, but when they were in the Gilded Globe, other than funny looks, little notes, and tiny pranks, Greg was all about the bartending staff. He was a bartender and that meant that his world sloshed and worked the bar. He didn't care what happened beyond the bar, but you mix up a drink or spill anything, then your ass was his. Thankfully, they never messed up and they had earned his friendship and his love.

Greg was a handsome man and he spent more time learning mixology and crafting his body into something that would make any woman turn to putty than anyone else in the bar. He was the kind of man that actually went to bartending conventions and learned the science behind mixing drinks and making sure that what he was serving was the very best. He'd been called an artist and he was drawing the attention of liquor connoisseurs all across the city and the coast.

He was one of the big pulls for the club and he was given a lot of authority and privilege to do what he wished and to sit when he worked. But, when you were the king of the bar, all you really wanted to do was work with friends and maintain the prime time and that was exactly what he did. He made sure that the girls worked the prime time just like he did and that was all they needed, a friend on the inside who loved them.

It wasn't hard to be friends with Greg. He was a bitter and sarcastic sort of soul who had filled the hole that his ex-fiancé had left in his heart with mixology and working out. He'd honed himself into a specimen that women envied and that got him laid as easily as it was for him to make a martini.

When Tara had shown up on the shores of the Gilded Globe, she thought that she was going to end up sleeping with Greg, but she quickly realized that Greg was a friend, not a boyfriend. His heart was given to one who had thrown it away and now he was without a heart.

He didn't sleep with fellow employees and he was kind enough to tell them that and give them the reason why. He wasn't interested in relationships that turned romantic. He was interested in being the best bartender on the east coast and getting laid every now and again. Tara was glad that she avoided that when he was first introduced to her.

Tina, however, would never give up on the hope of having Greg for her own and Tara had tried to dissuade her a thousand times, but she wouldn't hear it. Tina Rodriguez was the most beautiful Latina that you would find in the world and she worked as a model when she wasn't at the Gilded Globe and it was unsurprising that she was a huge success. With the right manager, she could do it full time, but she was more interested in partying and trying to convince Greg that they were soul mates.

Honestly, Tara could easily see them together and there was something that was extremely compatible between the two of them, but Tina was a victim of being around at the wrong time. If they stuck together and kept in each other's orbit, then they would eventually end up together. After all, they were part of the same pack and they were just a step above Tara in importance. They'd have each other soon, enough.

Tina was the kind of woman who put her mind to whatever her passion was at the time which was often fickle and tended to have her very well versed in a bunch of strange and interesting things that Tara had never even heard of, let alone dabbled in.

She was still taking classes at the local college and she was always looking for a new skill that she could take hold of and master. She was the kind of exciting woman who always had something that she could talk about and find common ground and relate to other people with. It was wonderful spending time with Tina and she was the most selfless and wonderful person that Tara had ever been given the opportunity to know and it made her a great mentor for this job.

When they first met and Tara realized how cool Tina was and how much she wanted to cling to Tina's side and stick with her. But, she was afraid that every new trainee would have the fantastic connection that she did with Tina and she knew that it was only a matter of time before that ended and that had always scared her. She had always been petrified of losing her friend, but that wasn't the case.

Tina and Tara were the two inseparable members of the serving staff and they were often mockingly called twins because they thought the same and they acted so similar when they were on the job. It wasn't until you dug deeper that you found that their spirits and actions were similar, but their history was completely different. Tara could only wish she was as adventurous and as outgoing as Tina.

"I'm not excited for this at all," Tina said nervously. "I hate it when we have Shifters here."

"I like it," Laura said with a shrug.

Of course she liked it. Laura was new to their little squad and she was quickly filling out to be her own person, but she was the only trainee that they had encountered who wasn't absolutely annoying and who wasn't gone in the blink of an eye. There was a special grit and gusto to Laura that kept her around and that they had kind of taken her under their wing.

Laura was new to the city and she was a lot like Tara when it came to the pack, but she was much more of a sympathizer and she was much more willing to bend the knee to the will of anyone above her. She would easily rise above Tara and Tina in a matter of no time and she would do it shamelessly and reap the untold rewards of it.

It was because of the fact that Laura knew what it was like to be a part of a fierce, large pack. She understood that there was a political game that was to be played with anyone who was looking to advance within the pack. She had the skills, the grace, and the beauty to make people feel endeared to her, but it was all an act.

It was the façade that Tina and Tara couldn't stand, but when you broke the perfect, plastic shell of Laura and really got to know her, that was the woman that Tina and Tara were fond of. Beneath her exterior, there was a romantic's heart that denied the cynical and the bitter reality that she was living.

If Tara had to think of one way that would accurately describe what it was like to be Laura, she thought that it would have to be an underwater volcano. The Shifter world was a cold, wet place surrounding Laura and she was molten lava; full of romance and hope that was immediately blasted by the cold dark world of the Shifter packs that hardened her.

They created this hard, fake exterior, but you could crack through it and you'd find the girl that secretly read poetry in the park and loved watching romantic comedies and drink fruity wine.

But, the moment you walked into a Shifter crowd, she would laugh at poets, drink foul beer, and only watch crass comedies or action movies to impress the potential mates that she could end up with. It was a shame, but it was the demands of the reality that she lived in. As far as Tara was concerned, Laura was simply doing what needed to be done and what was more realistically demanded of her.

Laura was a funny girl and since she was the youngest of the group, she tended to get picked on, but she was also the baby of the group and they were fiercely protective of her. No one had freedom to pick on her or be mean to her and God help anyone who tried to put a hand on her.

"Of course you would," Tara grinned and jabbed her elbow into Laura's side. "Hunting for your next husband?"

"You never know." Laura gave her a knowing grin. Right there, that was what was going to make Laura the kind of success that Tara and Tina never would be in the pack. They were going to be down on the bottom, falling for each other and those like them while Laura had her sights set on a world that was high above them and she had the ambition and knowledge to go for it. Tina and Tara were from small packs and didn't know what it was like to be part of a large pack, Laura did and she was set to play the game like an expert.

"Quiet down, everyone," Charlie said. She was a cold, serious woman who was well aware of the Shifter presence in this club and was one of the many humans who was a part of the world, serving out a life debt or something that was owed to her masters. She was a bitter and seriously grim woman, but she was beautiful and she was efficient, so she was Luke's number two. "Is everyone here? I don't want to waste any more time waiting for anyone."

"Start then," Greg said bluntly. "Teach them to be on time."

"Couldn't agree more," Luke said, his deep, rumbling voice was full of authority and it was the kind of power that made everyone turn and look at him, catching a glance of their well-dressed manager as he stepped out of his office and graced them with his grim, powerful presence. It was the kind of presence that made all of them uncomfortable and feel like they were in trouble. "Thank you for being on time," Luke said to all of them.

Luke was a legend in the Shifter community, but even here in the Gilded Globe, he was a legendary figure that towered above everyone else. He was a neutral figure in the community, one who liked to facilitate peace and fix problems without turning into a monster and killing people. It was why he and Grayson conducted so much business here and got along so well. It was their mutual respect for words and the power that they held that kept them in league with one another.

He stood before them all, looking down the table at his employees, most of them human, but the Shifters among him he lingered on for a fraction of a moment longer than the rest. Someone who didn't know that they were Shifters might see this as either disappointment or favoritism, but it couldn't be anything farther from the truth. They were conspirators together and he was establishing that they were here to make sure that the night things would go smoothly. He wanted to know that everyone was aware of how important today was.

His blonde hair was immaculately cut and cared for to the extent that Tara wondered if he had a stylist who worked for him. Or if he was actually in charge of his magnificent hair on his own, or if that was just how he naturally looked. His face was handsome, but the severity of his personality warped it and turned him into something more terrifying that he probably wanted to be.

She knew that he was married, but she had never seen his wife before. She wondered who the pack had set him up with and if she was as pretty and cold as her man was. Either way, she had a husband who was exquisitely dressed and who cared for his appearance very much.

"Today is a special occasion," Luke told them with his voice rolling across the banquet table with its high backed chairs and its multitude of employees sitting at it or lingering around it. "Our owner, Grayson Wilkes will be gracing us with several other high-profile dignitaries. It's going to be paramount that tonight goes as smoothly as possible, because while the VIP room will be occupied, Mr. Wilkes has invited many high profile guests to the club to celebrate the ringing in of the New Year with him and the other guests.

Essentially, everyone you are meeting tonight is going to be very wealthy, very famous, or very important to the community, so I want everyone to be on their top behavior and to make sure that everything runs smoothly. Tips will be large tonight, no doubt about it, and we are having only our must trustworthy and experienced members of the staff working. Those of you who were not on the list, unfortunately, you will not be reaping the benefits.

However, you will have the first pick to request a shift on Valentine's Day, should you like the opportunity to make up the tips that you missed out on. For being such excellent employees, Mr. Wilkes has asked me to extend an invitation to all staff members who are not working to come and enjoy the festivities. I would strongly advise you to politely refuse this offer, but you're free to do as you choose.

Greg, you have been advised to select your staff pick for the bar and I hope that you have chosen wisely. You will be working in the VIP bar and you will be making sure that everything goes smoothly there, first and foremost. I will have no mistakes and I will have nothing going wrong downstairs. Does your team have their assignments?"

"I've got everything squared away," Greg said with a grin. "Everything is going to be in good hands, captain."

"Good," Luke said, turning to look at Tina. His eyes were the kind of cold that gave ice its color. It sent a shiver down Tara's spine when he looked at them. "Tina, Tara, and Laura, the three of you will be working the VIP lounge tonight and when the meeting is concluded, you'll work the mezzanine or wherever Charlie would have you stationed."

"We'll discuss it when the time comes," Charlie said bluntly.

"Very well," Luke said as they all heard the front doors to the club open and everyone turned, craning their necks to see who it was that had so boldly come to interrupt the proceedings of the staff meeting. It was highly irregular for someone to show up late or to make an entrance through the front door like that, but there was something cold in the pit of Tara's stomach that told her she knew exactly who it was that was coming through that door.

"Without any further ado, Mr. Grayson Wilkes would like to address you and thank you for your service. He's also here to extend an invitation to those of you not working tonight. Again, I strongly suggest that you make plans elsewhere tonight."

"Nonsense," Grayson said, his voice strong and unwavering, rippling across the room like a wave of smooth, calming power. He was the kind of calm and cool that other people no doubt envied and wanted to be a part of. He was the kind of successful that other people tried to emulate and whenever they saw him, they saw a man with power and knowledge of how to wield it effectively without being a douche.

"All of you are invited, even those who were late to the staff meeting. I know that Luke can be a hard-ass and is probably doing his most to scare all of you off, but show up, please. Be my guest for the evening and give me a chance to show you what it's like to be a part of this amazing club. You'll get a unique glimpse of what it's like to be a guest."

"Thank you, sir," Johnny, the bouncer, said with a grateful smile.

Grayson looked at him with his pale brown eyes that looked more amber and more luminous than any eyes that she'd ever seen before. He had a kind of power and presence that made her nervous, but when those eyes flicked her direction she knew that she was going to blush.

His eyes lingered on her for a moment, frozen, as if they were captivated by the woman that he wanted but that he couldn't have. She felt like she was going to burn up in those eyes and that any second, people were going to guess that they'd been sleeping together, but she was grateful that they flicked away in a heartbeat.

It wasn't just the fact that he was easily the most handsome man in the history of men that she had ever seen, it was the fact that he was interested in her, something that came out of the blue. She remembered the first time she saw his dark hair, combed high and back, his clean-shaven face that accented his strong jaw and his perfect chin. He had powerful cheekbones and he had the appearance of a man who knew how to take care of himself. It was the appearance that she was completely overwhelmed with.

His body was framed by the muscular presence over a skeleton that was taller than most of the men that she had ever seen. He was the kind of man that would make anyone feel inferior and small. He was the kind of man that women wanted to have rip off their clothes and press his full, strong lips against their naked skin until the sunlight peeked over the horizon again.

When she thought about him, picturing his sculpted, athletic body underneath that black, three-piece suit, she felt hot and excited all over. She felt the familiar longing and the familiar urges coming up again. It was powerful and she knew that she couldn't resist him, even if she ever wanted to.

And why would she ever want to? She was the luckiest woman in the world to have him in her life and be interested in her. She wanted to have his affections, his secret kisses, and his powerful presence with her for the rest of her life. This wasn't something that she was willing to give up. This wasn't something that she wanted taken away from her

She was going to ride this train out to completion, until he was bored with her or until his wife found out and they both ended up dead. It was all she wanted. When she closed her eyes at night, she pictured him in the bed next to him, as she showered she remembered his warm presence, and when she saw her phone flashing, she prayed that it was him.

"I just want all of you to know that all of the clubs and places that I own, I truly do take most pride in the Globe," Grayson said with the kind of voice that was easy to dismiss as something that every owner and investor said. But, she knew as a fact that this was truly his most favorite.

He talked about the Globe with passion and with a kind of fervor that very few men talked about with anything that they loved. The fact that he was so emotional about the Globe was just another testament that this was going to be the place that he loved forever and that she was at the heart of it.

Sometimes, she dared to wonder how much of his love was for the building and how much of it was for her. The answer was something that she was too afraid to learn, ever. "I hope that tonight, we all walk away with our pockets a little fatter and with the person that we love most in the world. I want you all to know that I'm here for you and I'm very grateful that you're all here for me. After tonight, we're all going to have an amazing year and I'm very happy to be spending it at the Globe with the rest of you."

There was a ripple of applause and a few cheers as he smiled and took a step back, allowing Luke to take the center of their attention again and he did so with such a presence that they all felt the cold chill of his authority rippling over them, consuming them and freezing them in place as they looked up at him. He held their gazes with the kind of authority and power that they all came to understand that he alone held in their lives. Luke was above God, family, and country. If he told them to jump, they would all go lunging as fast and as high as they possibly could. It wasn't negotiable.

"Each of you, report to your supervisors for a brief rundown," Luke told them. "I want everyone to know the menu from cover to cover and I want you to know the specials that Greg has set up for everyone to enjoy. This is the most important night of the year. This is going to be the standard with which every other holiday and every other party in the city is going to be judged by for the rest of the year.

We are going to blow the minds of our attendants and that is going to send ripples and shockwaves throughout the entire city and all along the East Coast. They're going to be whispering and talking with each other in California about this party and I want all of you to make it the best night of our guest's lives. So, leave all your slacking, all your troubles, all your woes, and everything else at the door. When you step through those doors, you're mine and you know nothing other than the Gilded Globe. Understood?"

"Understood, Luke," they all chanted in unison for their fearless leader. He looked at them with a kind of contempt and respect that swirled together into some kind of strange new emotion that Tara had never seen before. This was an emotion that only Luke could properly master and though everyone on the staff had tried to mirror it, it was impossible to capture and practice. But, when he was certain that his minions were all set to their task, he turned from them and whispered with Grayson.

Tara stood with the rest of the serving staff and headed over to where Charlie was standing like a sculpture carved out of ice. It was hard to tell whether or not she was actually breathing, but it was safe to assume that she wasn't. She wasn't even human— which was saying a lot, especially when a Shifter said it. Handing out menus to each of her serving staff, she started by going over what was on the menu and what would be offered to the guests for the evening, but before she could get very far, they were interrupted.

"Tara," Luke said, cutting through the sea of faces. "Mr. Grayson would like a tour to inspect the VIP lounge. I have a call to take, so would you run up there and let him inspect it to his liking?"

"Yes, Luke," she said, nervously glancing at Grayson.

Shit.

CHAPTER THREE

She could feel the fear running down the back of her spine as she stepped away from the flock of serving staffers that was waiting for her. She could feel their eyes on her, studying her as if she were the chosen one being taken away to a world that was beyond them, that was more than they could ever hope for. She could feel the burn of those eyes on her back and it made her nervous. She didn't like the attention and as she followed Luke up the steps to tier two where Grayson held out his hand for her to shake, she felt like her whole body was crumbling.

"Grayson Wilkes," he said, keeping up the charade for everyone around them.

"Tara," she said nervously, playing along for the moment.

"Luke says you're one of the best," Grayson said with his smooth voice as he looked over at Luke who nodded in agreement with the statement that he definitely never made. There was no way that Luke was ever sentimental. She looked over at Luke and gave him an enormous grin, having him swallow the compliment was a gift that she hadn't expected to receive. This was something precious and wonderful. "I trust Luke with my life, but I'm quite particular about the layout of the VIP lounge and it's been a few months since I've stopped by other than to pop into Luke's office, so I'd like to go up and have a look around. You mind showing it off to me and taking some notes about what I need to have changed?"

"Absolutely, sir," Tara said with a grin. "Would you like to follow me?"

"Would I ever," he said with a charming grin that told her that everything was going to be perfect. There was really nothing for them to worry about and she was certain that she was going to be just fine today, so long as he was here to make sure that nothing could be whispered among the guests.

"If you'd like to follow me, sir," Tara said, rather than asked him to follow her. She shot a glance over at Tina and Laura who were staring with the rest of the servers trying their hardest to steal glances as they could spare them from Charlie.

She gave them a nervous and terrified look that set them at ease, but as she walked, she knew that this was a close call. He was getting desperate and that meant that he was getting sloppy. She didn't like this. If someone found out about this, then they were going to get discovered by Harriet and she would have them ground up into hamburger or something.

She led him to the spiral staircase that led up to the mezzanine and when they were safely away from the view of the staff that was downstairs, scattered across tier one and tier two, she could feel the isolation and it was making her heart beat faster and faster, just having him this close to her.

She could feel her excitement all over and her breathing was beginning to pick up. She had to try harder to keep it under control than she normally did. She always had this problem when he was around. It was like she was possessed when he was near her. It was startling that he had this power over her.

"You look lovely today," he said to her as they reached the top of the stairs and stepped out on the mezzanine. She hated it when he was nice to her like this. It was like there was no shame in him and that there was nothing that she could do to keep him contained. He was a wildfire that would spread all over her life and when she turned around and looked at him, she felt like she was being pulled toward him, like there was a magnetic bond between them. All she wanted to do was press herself against him and kiss his soft lips, to feel his warmth. But she knew that there were eyes everywhere and that this wasn't the place.

"I look like a whore," she said bluntly to him.

"Every man likes it when his woman shows off her assets now and again," he said with a charming sort of tone in his voice that almost made that sound romantic to her, but she knew better. She knew that there was nothing romantic about it. The only thing that he was capable of with her was lust and that made her depressed.

"Come and see me every other night, now and again," she told him with a heavy heart. "Besides, I'm sure your wife wouldn't like it if you were looking at the serving girls at one of your clubs."

"Harriet doesn't like a lot of things," he reminded her. There was a silence there that curdled her blood and made her nervous. She knew that he was miserable and the mentioning of his wife was enough to make her feel the shadow of her presence looming over them.

There would never be any escaping her while they continued in this foolish relationship. The truth was one day they were bound to get caught and she knew that it was going to be a dark and grim day. That would be the day that they were going to be pulled apart from each other. "Besides," he said, taking up the lead and heading across the walkway along the wall of the club, getting a clear view of the golden planet rotating above the dance floor. "I was just trying to pay you a compliment."

Tara always felt nervous crossing the dance floor and she knew that it was a ridiculous fear, but it was impossible for her to get over. It was something naturally terrifying to her, seeing the giant golden planet. She thought that it was going to plummet into the dance floor when she first started working here, but she'd slowly began to trust it. One day it might fall, but she doubted very much that she would be under it.

The VIP lounge was a large room with mirrors and television screens with plush leather couches all along the wall. The far wall was where the serving staff could have direct access to the kitchen and there was also a bar where Greg would be working solo that night. It was the kind of place where everyone usually ordered the same thing, they always wanted to have champagne and they wanted a lot of it.

It was the kind of place where everything was nice, state of the art, and it was definitely where they had invested most of their money. It was the room that everyone wanted to hang out in or to throw a private party in, but they couldn't even afford the deposit for the room. When they walked into the VIP lounge, the heavy black curtain fell behind them and secluded them.

It was then that she realized just how alone she was with him. She could feel the tension in the room, filling up like it was being piped in among them and that they were getting the fill of it. She looked at him and she watched him as he walked around the room, looking at it as if he were taking it in for the first time ever. He'd been in this room a thousand times and she knew, just as well as he did, that it was fully stocked with everything that he needed for the night. No, what he wanted had just come into the room with him and he was more than eager to try and get a chance to enjoy her.

"I've missed you, Tara," he said calmly, but there was something in his voice that resonated deep and sounded true to her. It didn't sound like a lie, something that she had been anticipating and it wasn't something that she had been expecting, either. She always built herself up to be more bitter and angry toward him than she actually was. She suspected the worst in him and she suspected that he was always going to just use her. But, there was something about him that made her feel loved and special when they were together.

She liked him a lot and she knew that if things were different and they'd been given the opportunity of having a normal life and they had met in the middle of the bustling world of New York City as humans, she would have done everything in her power to have him and keep him in her life. But that wasn't in the cards for her and she knew it. He was taken and he was her superior. That was the end of it. There was nothing that she could do to save herself from the grim reality that was facing her right now.

"I missed you too," she confessed, but the words felt empty, meaningless as she looked at him, wishing that he would give her something more than empty words. She took a step forward, wishing that she could fly away from this room and that she could never come back. She wasn't interested in this game and she wasn't interested in playing with him. She wanted to have a world with him that was their own and that was beyond the reach of anyone else, but she knew that it wasn't possible. There was no escaping the reality of where they were.

"I want you," he said to her, rather forthcoming and cutting to the point of what he was doing up here with her. She knew that he could give the command and she would have no choice but to give herself to him, but he wasn't that kind of man. No, he was the kind of man who wanted her to give him everything that she had because she liked him. It was how he had seduced her. He wasn't a man to wield his power. She honestly believed that he felt something for her, or they wouldn't have been here. Instead they were standing in a room, both of them crazy about each other, but unable to do anything but secret things in the shadows with each other.

He turned and looked at her, his face as serious as the statement that he'd made and she knew that she wanted him just as badly. She'd been craving him, aching for him since they'd last been together, but she'd been lying to herself, lurking in a world of denial as she tried to tell herself that she didn't want it. No, she knew that this was wrong, but she found herself taking a step toward him. She wanted this, she hungered for this and she was going to have it. She stood in front of him, putting a hand on his shoulder and leaning in.

When his lips were pressed to hers, she knew that there was something powerful in his presence, something that connected with her soul and made her heart sing. It was the way that his lips were powerful and hungry, but locked with a soft restraint that made him feel so warm and so strong. He was a powerful kisser and she knew that he was a natural lover. Everything was so effortless for him and that was where he truly thrived.

God, there were things that he could do to her that no other man could ever replicate. It was the poison of being with him. No other man could do, but she would never have him. So, in these moments, she didn't mind.

She felt his hand slipping between her thighs and sneaking up her short, white skirt and she knew that they didn't have time to play with each other, which was a shame. They never had the kind of time that they wanted to play with each other and get each other worked up. They had to make sure of what time they were given and right now, they only had a short time.

She moaned as he kissed her neck and made her want to scream at the feeling of his lips pressing against her neck. His fingers worked diligently, running over the slit of her pussy and she knew that there was something magical in the way he made her feel so alive and so powerful with just his fingers. When he pushed aside her thong, she felt his fingers run down to the threshold of her pussy and he could feel how wet she truly was.

"You seem excited," he grinned at her.

"Lick me," she said, wrapping her fingers around his neck and whispering into his ear as he slipped his fingers inside of her and she gasped in the power of it running through her body. She wanted him so badly.

"My pleasure," he told her with a smile on his lips, kissing her softly once more on the lips and dropping to his knees as he lifted her up onto the bar. She braced herself and felt him hike her skirt up and looked at her pussy like a ravenous child in a candy shop, trying to figure out what it was that he was going to enjoy first. Pushing her thong aside, he brazenly ran his tongue up her slit and circled her clit, making her feel like her elbows were going to buckle and stop bracing her.

She held strong, biting her lower lip as he worked her clit, knowing that there was no way that she could scream or moan like she wanted to. His tongue rubbed against her clit, soaking her and massaging her as she writhed and could feel her hips working with him, rocking back and forth as her body begged for more and more. She knew that there was nothing more incredible in the world than being licked by him. The way his tongue moved and it massaged her, it was impossible not to get addicted to him.

His tongue worked miracles on her and as she moaned and closed her eyes, trying her hardest to let go of everything. There was nothing that she wanted more than to grip his head, pull it toward her pussy, and scream at the top of her lungs as the orgasm built up heavier and heavier inside of her.

It swelled, roaring to life like a great storm from deep inside of her, conjured up and drawn out by his tongue as she wrapped her fingers around the back of his neck and pulled him closer and closer, hissing to keep the moans silent. She couldn't run her fingers through his hair like she wanted to and she couldn't scream, but she would have him close to her.

When the orgasm hit, pulsing through her and vibrating through and all over body and through each and every cell of her body, she threw back her head and mouthed a silent scream, keeping it caged up inside of her, locked away so that no one else could hear her lust take form and sound. She pinched her eyes shut and felt him kissing the insides of her thigh as he stood up and leaned over her, pressing his wet lips to hers and she could taste everything that she wanted. She could taste him, herself, and everything in between, it was the melding of them and she loved feeling his lips on hers.

The orgasm rocked her world and as he kissed her, she licked his lips, pulling his tongue out, coaxing it out to dance with hers and as they pressed together, she could feel the heat of the moment swirling around her, filling her with the life that she longed for with him.

It was a glimmer of another world where they were together and this was the passion that she would receive on a daily basis, a hint of the hope that she had. When she opened her eyes, she clamped her hands on the sides of his face and held him close, kissing him tenderly as their tongues played with each other.

She wanted his lips on hers for the rest of her life and she was going to be sad when there was nothing left for her. There was going to be nothing for her but the loneliness of not having him. But she wouldn't let that keep this moment from escaping her.

Her fingers were nimble and they were spritely. They danced over his belt and unbuckled it with the finesse of a woman who was truly talented, unzipping him and unbuttoning him as she pulled him down and revealed his cock trapped inside of his underwear. She ran her fingers over it, rubbing it hard and feeling the familiar strength of it.

Oh God, she wanted him inside of her. He was long and thick, the kind of cock that women only got to experience if they went out and bought a plastic version of it. She loved his cock so much and as she slipped her fingers under the band of his underwear and felt how hot it was, how strong it was, and how hard it was, she couldn't help but squeeze it, testing its strength and enjoying every second of it. Yes, this was the cock that she wanted inside of her right now and for the rest of her days.

"Quickly," she whispered, leaning her forehead against his and feeling their warm, frantic breath mingling passionately, hungrily. "Quickly, I want you inside of me."

"Someone might discover us," he whispered, playing with her and teasing her. She knew that even if Luke walked in on them, there was no way that Luke would ever tell. There was enough money and power in Grayson to scare the entire world into silence. She smiled at him and knew that he was playing, but with her fingers wrapped around his cock, she knew that she was in charge.

She pulled him closer to her, letting the tip of his cock play with the lips of her pussy, teasing him and sending the excitement shooting through him. She knew that he was just as hungry as she was. They both wanted this so badly.

"God, you're incredible," he whispered to her, slowly pushing his cock against the threshold of her pussy and trying his hardest not to moan and shudder with the euphoria that was running through him right now. She knew that there was no escaping it. She could feel it rushing through her as well. "You're everything I've ever wanted in a woman," he closed his eyes and let his cock slide deeper and deeper inside of her.

She took him into her and she felt him pushing deeper and deeper inside of her. She opened her mouth and clamped her hand over it, refusing to let the shuddering scream that was deep inside of her escape. She wasn't going to give away anything that was happening in this room. There were no cameras, no witnesses, and there was no one to tell. She was going to keep this their little secrets.

But, as he pushed deeper and deeper inside of her, she knew that she was never going to get used to how powerful he was and how strong his cock was. It was so big and perfect that there was truly no way of getting used to it. She wondered if Harriet had gotten used to it, or if they even had sex anymore.

She didn't care, she dug her fingernails into him as he pushed deeper and deeper inside of her, his balls slapping against her ass as she moaned and took him entirely into her. He gave her another thrust, pushing in as deep as he could and she let out a sharp, stunted yelp as a smile spread across her lips.

She knew that he was trying to get her to scream. It was a dangerous game, but as she ran her fingers through the back of his hair, it was a fun game that they played often. Whenever they were secretly meeting and stealing a moment for each other, he always tried to get her to give up everything and let the world know about them. She knew that secretly, he probably wanted to get caught so that he could have her to himself once and for all, but Tara wasn't so foolish.

He slipped his cock out of her until only the head was inside of her, dangerously close to slipping out and she smiled as he rammed inside of her again and began to fuck her with the kind of speed and force that was demanded of their haste. She rocked her hips, moving in rhythm with him as he took her and dug in as deep and as furious as he could.

Her whole body was trembling and shaking as she dug her fingers into the back of his head and into his shoulder, the whole bar felt like it was rocking and shaking as he fucked her furiously, taking out all of the built up lust and longing that he had for her. She could feel the swell of the new orgasm building up, layering the tingling, and quivering sensation of what was left over her.

It was growing, rising and building as she smiled and felt him taking her in and causing her to bite her lower lip, sinking deeper and deeper into the vibrations that were picking her up and filling her with everything that she ever wanted. She knew that this was the greatest lie that she ever told herself, but she couldn't help but feel like this was destiny. This was everything that she ever wanted to have and that it was so fortunate that she'd ever had the chance to meet him. This was all that she wanted. This was all that she hungered for.

When he came inside of her, she smiled and moaned softly, grinding her hips against him as he held her tightly and unloaded everything that he had inside of her. She smiled and looked at him, gazing into his eyes and knowing that this was something that she could never hold onto. It was already a memory and that made her sad.

She was never good at hiding her emotions and even as the orgasm was rippling through her body like a tsunami rushing over her, she knew that there was something horrible that she was never going to be able to recover from.

She looked away from his bright, hazel eyes and didn't dare look him in the eye again. There was no way that she was going to be able to look at him and give him what she wanted to give him. There was no way that she was ever going to be sincere for him and that he was going to be sincere with her.

This was all just an illusion that they were sharing and that they were partaking in. This was the great lie that they drank deep of when they were together, but the moment it was over, the depression came sweeping in like a dark cloud on a stiff breeze.

She didn't bother watching him as he leaned over the bar and grabbed a pair of napkins and gave her some. She took them graciously and started to clean herself up, trying her hardest not to react to the moment where he pulled the head of his cock out of her, but it was too powerful. It really was just too much for her not to wince and smile at the power of it. He grinned and chuckled at the sight of her in such an uncomfortable and lustful moment of weakness, but the smile faded from her lips faster than it had been there.

"What's wrong?" he asked her after a moment.

"Nothing," she whispered back to him. She went about cleaning herself up and she knew that he was watching her, his eyes on her for a long time, feeling her for more than what she was saying. He was probing her, studying her for every little sign and every little reading that he could get from her, but she wasn't giving it up. She wasn't going to give him a single thing and she knew that there was very little that she could give him right now that would make him happy. If anything, the more he looked at her, the sadder he was going to become.

"Come on," he said, taking a step forward and kissing her on the forehead. She loved the feeling of his lips pressed against hers, the smell of his cologne, and the warmth radiating from his chest and his arms, but it was killing her inside. How long had they been doing this? How long had they been pretending like this was fine and that there was nothing happening between the two of them? "Talk to me, Tara," he pressed.

"I'm just a stupid girl," she said, trying her hardest not to cry. "When we started this, I knew that it was just going to be us hooking up together and that this was never going to go anywhere. I knew that we were just a fling and that this was nothing more than sex, but I couldn't keep that promise to myself."

"What do you mean?" he asked her softly.

"I think I'm falling for you, Grayson," she said, pushing back from him and standing up, taking the napkins from him and throwing them away, stuffing them deep in the trash so that no one could ever find them. There was no way that they were ever going to get caught on her watch. Sure, there was probably a deep part of Grayson's mind where he wanted to just give up on the whole charade, but she wasn't.

She felt something grab her arm and she turned around, spinning with the force of the hand and she found herself smashed against Grayson, their lips locking and kissing again. His hand pressed against her cheek and held her close to his face as he kissed her intimately, making sure that she was fully aware of how he felt about her. She smiled at the sensation of his kiss. This was the heaven that she wanted.

"I'm already fallen," he confessed to her with such a feeling of wonder that she found it hard to breathe as the words escaped his lips. There was no recovering from that sort of a confession and she felt her whole life flashing before her eyes. "Harriet was a decision that I didn't make and you know that I'm not any happier with her than she is with me, but don't for a second think that I take this lightly.

I think you're the most incredible woman that I've ever met and I don't think that you're just some bimbo that I fuck on the side. You're the woman that I want to spend my days with, Tara. You're the woman that I want to share dinner with and hear about your day. You're the woman that I want nothing but great and wonderful things to happen to. You're my girl, Tara. You're the woman that I've wanted forever."

She kissed him and while she knew that it was a nice sentiment, it was nothing more than trivial sentimentality. There was no way that they were going to ever have the chance to have anything more than precious words with each other and locked away emotions that they were never going to be able to let come out and play in the light of day. That only depressed her more. She didn't want to think about it anymore, so she kissed him and did so as if it were the last time that she was ever going to get the chance to see him.

"You should get back downstairs," she whispered to him softly. "I'll clean up here."

"I'll see you tonight," he promised her, but she knew that all they would share would be secret glances at one another and nothing more. There was no way that she was going to be able to spend any time with him. There was no way that she was going to be able to dance with him or to hold him or kiss him as the New Year rang in. She smiled at him and nodded. Yeah, he would see her and he would pretend that there was nothing between them and Harriet would probably get suspicious, just like she always did, even if Tara wasn't there.

He pushed back the curtain and headed off to the mezzanine and to the stairs that would lead him all the way back to where Luke would be hanging out, waiting to see if there was anything that he wanted to change. Grayson would tell him something bogus or point out a few things, but it would be nothing substantial. It would be the kind of trivial stuff that would throw off suspicion about what they'd been doing for the past ten minutes.

She turned to the counter and started cleaning it, getting rid of any sign that she had just made love to the man that she was totally smitten for and that she was obsessed with. It was hard, but she knew that there was nothing waiting for her here. She knew that there was nothing but disappointment and work. One day, she would hopefully have a man who was a fraction of the grandeur and greatness that Grayson was, but until then, she knew that she would just end up pining for him.

CHAPTER FOUR

They all had a brief break before the club officially opened to receive guests. There would be a few people who showed up early, but there would never be much until it hit around seven or eight o'clock. It was a long time until the clock struck midnight, but they had to be back at six. When Tara, Tina, Laura, and Greg all went to grab dinner before the festivities, she couldn't help but think about how much fun the evening was going to be and how insane the night was going to be.

New Year's Eve was usually a difficult night, because there was plenty of alcohol flowing, but rarely was it anything spectacular. Most people wanted champagne and most people wanted a few cocktails at first, but when people were all well-lubricated, it became a drag.

The staff had fun, making their rounds, chatting with guests, and getting the tips that would set them up for the rest of the month, but in the end, it kind of felt like an overly-glorified regular night.

So, when they arrived at the Gilded Globe, everyone was getting back at the same time and they were all making last minute changes. Women were adjusting their make-up, stuffing their bras, making sure that they looked as lusty and alluring as they possibly could be for the throngs of people who were going to storm the club and expect to be treated like the kings that they were most definitely not. She didn't feel anything but disdain for the night because she was going to be up in the VIP lounge with the others.

"To your positions," Luke clapped his hands as they unlocked the doors and started letting in the first of the guests. The DJ was already drowning out the club with the kind of music that had to be custom made, spliced and crafted to earn him a paycheck that distinguished him from the thousands of other DJs in the city.

Surprisingly, Tara never really noticed the music. It was always something loud and something that got people onto the dance floor. The DJ was talented, but she had it fairly easy tonight. She got free drinks, played recordings she'd already made, and got hit on by the thousands of guys that were eager to flirt with her.

"Ready or not, here we come," Laura said as they walked through the kitchen and walked up the spiral staircase that led up to the VIP lounge. When they reached the top of the stairs, they walked through a small room tucked behind the bar that gave them easy access to silverware or condiments that the guests might like, they walked into the VIP lounge and watched as Greg manned the station.

"Feels good to be home," he said with a mischievous grin.

Tina and Tara turned the TVs all on to something different so that the guests could pick what they were watching. If they were seated in a place that wasn't showing what they were interested in, they could look at the mirrors and see something different that they wanted to watch.

"It's going to be hours before they show up," Tina moaned, taking a seat at the bar as Tara opened up the curtains and linked the velvet ropes that made it feel even more exclusive. Someone had to man the VIP entrance until the guests showed up and they would all take shifts for about a half an hour at a time or as long as they wanted to.

Tara found herself excited and eager to take up the post. She had spent most of the day moping around and depressed that she wasn't going to get to spend the time with Grayson, but now she was eager to see him. She wanted to see what he was wearing to the New Year's party. He had the best sense of fashion and style that she'd ever seen.

"What were you two talking about up here earlier?" Greg called out to Tara who turned around and felt her heart pounding. She looked at him and wondered if there was something that he knew that she didn't know. She tried her hardest to maintain a sense of calm, but she knew that something was up.

"Nothing really," she said honestly. They hadn't been doing a lot of talking when they were up here, but she wasn't going to elaborate. Of course, she knew that they wanted her to elaborate, so she decided to make something up. She had to satiate the curiosity before it became something more. "He just wanted to see what the bar was stocked with. He was really particular about everything. It was kind of weird."

"What?" Greg frowned. "This is the best stocked bar in New York City. I guarantee that if you go to any other club, you're not going to find what we have in our VIP lounge anywhere else, let alone in their crappy VIP areas. The man's paranoid."

"I think he likes you," Laura said with a smirk on her lips. That bothered her even more. She didn't like it when rumors like this started to pop up. She gave Laura a scowl and that was all that she had to do to make Laura question her. "Hey, I'm just saying. I think that it's kind of suspect that he calls you out to take him on the tour. I bet he was checking you out the entire time."

"He's married," Tina said resolutely. "And if he wife hears you saying that or even thinking that, she'll kill you, Tara, and Grayson for even having that thought in your head."

"You know Harriet?" Tara asked. She'd never been to any of the pack meetings. She didn't rank high enough to get a chance to show up and listen to the politics of what was happening, but she'd heard rumors. This was going to be the first time that she actually saw Harriet, especially with the man that she was married to. She felt nervous about that. What if she could smell him on her?

"I've seen her a couple times," Tina said.

"She's kind of a bitch," Greg added.

"Kind of," Tina laughed.

Tara decided that she wasn't going to broach the subject further and she wanted to keep silent as she looked across to the mezzanine. The hours trickled by and when it got to around nine o'clock, the first person to arrive on the mezzanine level with an intent to walk over to the VIP lounge drew Laura's attention, who was on watch.

She snapped her fingers and everyone in the room stood at attention, eager to serve and do whatever was needed to be done. This was where they were supposed to shine. Tara stood up straight and off to the side with a false smile on her face that looked as close to real as possible.

The man walked past Laura and into the room. He looked at Greg, clearly taking the man as the one in charge. "I talked to Luke, they're coming," the man said it as he took a seat at the bar and made sure that his task of alerting the staff was done.

"Can I get you anything?" Greg asked him. "It's on the house."

With that little adage at the end, the man adjusted his tie nervously and nodded. "Get me a bourbon, two fingers," his eyes darted over to Tara and looked her up and down. "Nice legs, sweetheart."

His words were like firebrands sticking into her and she hated them, but she shut off her brain and locked away her soul like she did every time she was on shift here. "Thanks," she said with a smile that he bought as genuine as she made her way over to the entrance to help Laura with the jackets and coats.

It wasn't long before the rest of the Shifters showed up, the pack that Tara was a part of, but rarely got to see. They were the largest and most dangerous-looking men that she had ever seen. All of them were wolves, just like she was. They could turn into the most vicious, feral creatures at the snap of a finger and she knew that there was no escaping them if you made them mad.

Of course, that was when she saw Grayson, walking in, wearing a white suit that made him look truly amazing. There were seven in total and she helped Laura take their coats as they entered the VIP lounge and took their places around the room. Most of them were here as bodyguards and that was their only point for being here.

Harriet was the glittering jewel of the room and she was every bit as beautiful as Tara had imagined her and it made her nervous just looking at her. She had straight blonde hair that hung over her shoulders and the face of an angel that would make any man fall in love with her in a second. Her lips were crimson red and her eyes were bright sapphires, alive and dancing in the lights of the room.

Her silver, sequined dress glittered and shined, hugging her lovely, lithe body like it had been poured on her, running over her exquisite curves and coating her in the most glorious silver. She looked around the room, eyeing the three women who were here to serve.

"Shifters?" she asked them.

All of them nodded.

"Good," she said sternly, her voice like shattering glass. "You're not to mention anything that you see here tonight. Forget it the moment we walk out. Is that understood?"

"Understood," they all repeated in unison. They knew the drill.

The men who showed up were towering figures and it was rather quickly established that they were bear Shifters. They were the second largest pack in the whole city and they were dangerous. There was a history between the two packs that Grayson wanted to bury the hatchet on and end once and for all. The five of them that entered the room were friendly and they had left their women back at the mezzanine.

Tara didn't hesitate to serve the drinks that they all ordered. Greg whipped them up expertly and with the kind of speed and skill that was expected of him. She smiled and played along as the men smiled at her, flirted with her, and stared a little too long at her cleavage. But she was good. She didn't look at Grayson and she didn't act suspicious around them. She just played along like a good little bottom rung Shifter was supposed to.

For the next hour, they negotiated and hammered out something that didn't make any sense to her. It was the kind of discussion that she knew that she wasn't supposed to understand, but it was too hard for her follow along, anyway. She just stood back and took glasses from anyone who was finished and would take a drink to anyone who needed more. As they talked and argued about what was happening in the politics of the packs, Tara just pretended like it was a different language to her.

Whatever it was that was so important to them, there was something in it for Harriet and that was what drew the most of Tara's attention. She thought that it was odd that Harriet was so interested in the politics of the pack which seemed to be so wrapped up in the world of the male Shifters. There were even points that she was contradicting and butting heads with Grayson who was trying his hardest to make things transition as peacefully and as calmly as possible, but she wouldn't have anything of the proposition.

Eventually the deal was struck and while both parties didn't seem entirely satisfied with the other half of the party, she knew that there was something substantial that was built here, something that was quality and that they were going to look back on with pride and the happiness, that they were all going to enjoy in the end. That was the glory and the respect that was given to Grayson when he came together with a deal. He was a man who liked to see that things were done right and everyone walked away with something.

"When I heard about you," the largest bear named Ryan stood up and held up his glass of whiskey, "I thought that you were a dandy and that there was nothing that we could solve or come to terms with. I used to tell my friends that you were going to be the downfall of you wolves, but I understand now.

Time and time again, I've watched as more and smaller packs have negotiated peace treaties and tried to get themselves in with you, nice and solid. I get that now and I'm glad that we won't be going to war with each other any time soon. I know that your father is a hard man and that he's not one to cross, but I'm sure that we'll be able to have peace together if the two of us keep working together like this."

"I'm glad that we could come to terms with each other," Grayson said, standing up and holding up his glass to Ryan's and willing to join in friendship with their new alliance. "There's no reason that we should be at each other's throats. We have enough problems as Shifters and we don't need to be enemies.

I refuse to think that there is nothing inside of us other than barbaric hatred that we've been told to have since we were children. We can overcome our antiquated traditions and rise above the beastly nature inside of us. So, here's to a successful and a long lasting friendship between our two packs."

"I'll drink to that," Ryan said with a grin spreading across his lips.

There was a cheer that rose up from all of the people present and Tara couldn't help but feel like she was witnessing something special, like this was a moment that was going to live on and that was going to last for a very long time. People were going to be talking about this for years to come, but she knew that there was something more in the words of Grayson.

There was hope and there was belief in them. He really did want to break down the traditions that kept them in the past—the traditions that kept him from being with her. She knew that it was foolishness to believe that there was ever going to be a world where they could get together and be a couple, but she could dream and she wasn't going to hold herself back.

His eyes flashed to her and she didn't smile at him, she didn't react to it, and she didn't do anything, because she knew that Harriet had caught the little darting of his eyes. She knew that Harriet's cruel, frigid graze was lingering on her and that if she showed any sign of weakness or if she showed any sign of affection for Grayson that she was going to end up dead or she was going to be banished from the pack. She needed the safety they offered her and she needed the hope that they provided to her. There was no living in a world without a pack.

Finally, when Harriet's gaze left, passing back to Grayson who extended his hand to his wife and invited her to stand with him, Tara watched Harriet, studying her sharp, beautiful features and wishing that it was her who was standing next to Grayson with his arm slipping around her lower back, hugging her close to his body. God, she wanted that in her life and she wanted to hold it close to her. But, she knew that there was never going to be that opportunity in her life and she pushed the folly aside.

But she couldn't.

Not tonight.

She watched as Grayson took a drink from his own cocktail and turned, kissing Harriet on the lips and it was the kind of passionate lip lock that she knew that she wanted right now. She wanted those lips on her lips and she wanted him to draw her hand up instinctively, just like Harriet's was as it brushed his cheek and cupped his face, holding him close to her.

Tara watched at Harriet leaned in, her breasts pressing against Grayson and there was an image of them together, an image of them happily together as a married couple should be and it horrified her. It was the kind of image that she knew that she was never going to be able to get out of her mind. To someone who had no idea about the things that Grayson had told her about his wife, one might think that this was a happily married couple and that they had the stuff to carry them through for the rest of their lives.

But she knew better. She knew that Grayson was a cheater and that she was jealous of the woman that he was married to. Even if this was a show that was being put on for the rest of the world, it was convincing and it broke her heart. It was like watching the world that she had pictured and that she had hoped for in her life bursting into flames and dying right in front of her.

There was no getting back what it was that she wanted and there was no reclaiming it now. She knew that there was nothing that she could ever have, right now, that she wanted. She was going to live a life alone in the shadow of the pack, dreaming of something that she could never have.

"Tara, are you okay?" Tina whispered to her. Her voice was barely above a hiss, worried and fearful as she leaned in close and pulled Tara away.

"I'm fine," Tara said, her voice quivering and cracking.

"You're crying," Tina told her. "Go clean yourself up before anyone notices."

Lifting a hand, she wiped a tear that had escaped from her eyes. She felt nervous, looking at the cold tear on the tips of her fingers. She wasn't herself. There was something wrong right now.

CHAPTER FIVE

When the last of the wolves and the bears left the VIP lounge, Grayson gave them the word that they could close up and that they were done with the VIP lounge for now. Laura was given the shift of lingering if anyone needed their coats or if they wanted to come back and share a drink with someone that they found on the dance floor or down below. It was likely that everyone was going to end up never coming back until they needed their coats to leave, but even then, they could ask for it downstairs and they would get it to them. Right now, all they had to worry about was getting someone to kiss when the midnight hour came.

As for Tara, she was done. "I don't feel well," Tara said to Tina as they walked down the steps into the kitchen. She needed to get out of here. It felt like the walls were coming in on her about to crush her at any second. She couldn't catch her breath and suddenly, she felt like she was going to throw up.

She couldn't handle this and she needed to get away. There was something inside of her that triggered the moment she saw that Harriet and Grayson were together and it felt like her soul had been crippled, like there was a shot taken at her and there was no escaping it. There had been something unleashed inside of her.

"You don't look so hot either," Tina said, her voice more worried than insulting, which was good, because under different circumstances, Tara would have blown up about that comment. "Get out of here and I'll cover for you. We only have an hour and a half until midnight. We've already got the champagne covered and I'll make sure that Charlie doesn't notice that you're gone."

"Thank you," Tara said with an exhausted exhale. "I'll let you keep my tips."

"No way," Tina said, shaking her head. "I'll drop them off for you tomorrow."

"Thanks," Tara said again, cutting through the kitchen and hacking through the mob of people. She felt like she was going to throw up if she didn't get out of the sea of gyrating bodies and the humid air that smelled like sweat, lust, and excitement.

She fought her way home to the street where she put on her coat and walked a few blocks, trying to catch her breath before she hailed a cab to take her home. It was miserable right now and she felt like there was no escaping this feeling that was inside of her.

She couldn't breathe and she couldn't escape it. She wanted to just scream at the top of her lungs and she knew that there was nothing that she could do to be free of it. This was the worst feeling that she had ever experienced before and there was nothing that she could do to let it relent. It was like getting hit by lightning over and over again.

When she made it home, she could hear the thumping of other rooms where the music was turned up all the way and people were hosting their own makeshift raves and parties that would get them in trouble any other night. She rode the elevator up to her floor and stepped out nervously, glancing at the end of the hallway where a dark room was pulsing and black lights were illuminating something that looked dangerously close to an orgy as people danced in practically nothing, swinging glow sticks and flashlights. A man turned and looked at her for a moment, wondering if he would be so lucky to have her come join the fun. She offered him an apologetic no and stepped into her apartment and closed the door behind her, locking it.

It didn't take long for her to tear off her clothes and to heap them in a pile in the corner of her room, pretending that there was nothing left for them and that this was the last time that she was ever going to squeeze back into them. She knew that it was a lie, just like she knew that her hopes and dreams were a lie.

There was no escaping the truth and as she stood in her panties, she took them off and tossed them in the pile and pulled on a pair of black panties that she would sleep in tonight. Pulling on a long sweatshirt and a pair of long socks, she decided that the rest of the night was going to be spent on the couch with a carton of ice cream, watching Netflix. She would be celebrating this year alone and she would have it no other way. She wouldn't be disturbed and she wouldn't be bothered.

It was an hour later and she realized that she wasn't feeling her ice cream at all. In fact, it was making things worse and she found that it was the strangest sensation that she was having. All she wanted to do was relieve all the pain and the frustration that she was having, but she didn't know what to do.

She felt like she was going insane and the apartment was strangely hot. Glancing out the window, she saw that the apartment across the alley was illuminated by a TV screen and an older woman was sitting in a chair, watching whatever program she was captivated by. Tara realized that the woman with her face scarred by wrinkles was her future and that she was going to end up miserable and alone for the rest of her days. It was like looking through a time machine.

She jumped at the sound of a knock on her door and she knew that it was probably the guy who was interested in her earlier. She quietly drifted across the carpet of her apartment, avoiding all of the squeaky places that revealed her movements all the time. She had adapted to the apartment and she knew where everything was. She wasn't going to be given away this time.

As she walked toward the door, she fought the conflicting emotions inside of her. She knew that the guy down the hall was probably stoned out of his mind, but it would be a nice revenge fuck to get back at Grayson, but there was a part of her mind that was fiercely loyal to him and wouldn't hear anything of the sort. She knew that there was no escaping it. She was in love with him and he was using her as a mistress.

Standing on the tips of her toes, she peeked through the peek hole and saw that there wasn't a stoner standing on the other side of the door. In fact, it didn't look like anyone from the rave and that disturbed her. The man on the other side of the door was handsome and charming-looking, the face of a man that she knew that she was putty and worthless in front of.

She felt a sinking feeling in her stomach, like this was the moment where he told her that they were through and that he had reconciled with his wife. This was the moment that she was kicked out of the pack. That was fine, she wasn't sure that she wanted to be a part of their stupid club anymore, anyways.

She opened the door and left the chain in place, glaring at him as he stood in front of her. God, he looked as handsome as a hero, he might as well be dressed in shining armor right now. She could feel herself getting lustful. She could feel the dark feelings of moist kisses and hot tongues slithering into her mind and she knew that she couldn't resist him.

"What do you want?" she asked him bluntly, not interested in talking with him.

"I noticed that you weren't at the party," he said with a crooked smile that sliced through to her heart. "I got worried that you saw something that you didn't like, or didn't trust."

"You mean you and Harriet?" she asked, cutting to the chase. "You're a married man, Grayson. You're a happily married man and your wife seems to love you very much. I'm not going to be a home wrecker. I'm not going to destroy your marriage just because you want a little side action. I thought that you loved me. How stupid was I?"

"Of course it looked like that," he hissed at her, his eyes glancing down the hallway to the rave that was happening. She knew that he was uncomfortable and that he was in a building that his father owned. There was a good chance that one of the stoners down the hallway was a Shifter and that he or she was going to recognize the man standing outside of Tara's door. "Look, let me come in and talk to you. I know that you're upset, but I'm going to make things up to you, I promise you."

"I don't want to talk to you," Tara told him sternly. "I know what I saw and I'm not going to be your mistress."

"If you were just a piece of action I was getting on the side, then why am I here right now?" He asked her. "Do you realize that I'm putting everything at risk by coming here right now? Tara, I'm in love with you and I'm not afraid to say it. My marriage to Harriet has to look sincere, or people will begin to doubt the pact that it signifies. I like her as much as I'd like to hug an eel."

No, that was not what Tara wanted to hear. She didn't want to hear that he loved her and that this was all a sham. She closed the door and unlatched the chain, letting him come into her small, cramped apartment. When he stepped in, he quickly shut the door behind him and locked it. When he turned around and got a glimpse of what his mistress was living in, she knew that he was shocked by it.

"Like it?" She asked him cynically. "It's the finest that the bottom feeders in the pack get to enjoy."

"This seriously can't be what you're living in," he said, baffled by the look of the room.

"It's not that bad, once you get used to it," she shrugged. She knew that Tina and Laura were in similar situations. For what she was paying for this apartment monthly, she could buy a house anywhere else. New York City was one giant joke after another. She just didn't realize it yet. "We can't keep doing this," she said finally, feeling like it had to be said. "We can't keep playing with each other and toying with each other's emotions. I'm already hurt and it's only a matter of time before you end up hurt."

"Give me some time," Grayson took a step forward, taking off his white jacket and tossing it over the back of a chair. "I'm going to tear down the whole system. I'm going to do away with the archaic traditions that we have. I want everything to be new and everything to be different. The way we've been living is stale and old. I don't want our people to live like animals anymore. There are too many worthless people in positions of authority and power and too many good people on the bottom. Harriet goes against everything I stand for t and when my parents relinquish power to me, I know that she'll challenge me. Once she's gone, I'm going to marry you, Tara. I'm going to make sure that you're my wife. I want you by my side and I want Harriet gone."

"Don't say that," Tara shook her head. She didn't want to hear it. She couldn't bear to get her heart broken like this. She couldn't be wrapped up in the toying games that would render her heart and destroy her. She needed to take care of herself. She needed to make sure that she was watching out for herself. This couldn't be how she ended up, hurt and broken again.

"I will," he promised her. "You saw her tonight. She wants to be in charge and she wants the power for herself. She hates that I'm progressive and she's a staunch traditionalist. It's going to lead to conflict and I'm going to dissolve the marriage pact between us. All I need is some time to make sure that other marriages are arranged so that her father can't pull his old pack away. All I need is a little more time."

She looked at him, her eyes full of fury and she shook her head. She couldn't wait. She couldn't do this to herself. All she wanted was to have him in her bed next to her and to have him by her side. She wanted to make love to him every night and she wanted to give him everything that he could desire, but she also wanted everything from him. She didn't want to play second fiddle anymore.

But honestly, as she looked at him, she understood that this was the truth. She had seen him there last night and she had seen exactly what it was like for him to be with her. There was no hope for the two and it would only be a matter of time before their entire relationship ended up as a fraud and its destruction was inevitable. No doubt, Harriet was making her vile little plans as well, and that meant that she was a dangerous person right now. If Harriet found out about them, then she would strike first. She could never find out about them.

But at the same time, Tara needed to know that this wasn't all lip service. She didn't want to be a pawn and she wanted to know once and for all that she was going to be the person that he ended up with and that he was with her. She took a step toward him and she slipped her fingers between the fold of his shirt, slipping between the buttons and clenching his shirt tightly. When she ripped, the sound of buttons popping was music to her ears.

There was a horrified expression on his face and she knew that this was going to be the test. If he loved her and wanted her, he would pleasure her then and he would give her everything that she demanded. If he was using her, then he would be furious at her and he would make a fuss about it. Either way, she was going to have an answer to her dilemma and her heart was going to be set at ease once and for all. She wasn't going to play this game anymore. She wasn't going to destroy her heart.

"What are you doing?" He grinned, looking at the ruins of his shirt and smiling at her.

"Take off all your clothes," she demanded of him, turning around and pulling her sweater off, letting him look at her delectable ass as she revealed her back and felt the frigid air kissing her hot skin. She felt hotter than normal, like there was something wrong with her, like she had a fever or something. She could hear him complying behind her as she let her hair down and turned to look at him. "Am I going to be your queen, then?" she asked him, walking one foot in front of the other toward him, her nipples standing alert and ready for him as he looked over her naked, perfect body. She could feel his eyes lustfully eating her up and she could see that he was practically drooling at the sight of her in her black panties and her black long socks. She wanted to get everything that she could from him.

"You'll be my everything," he promised her, kicking off his briefs and standing in front of her completely naked, his cock erect and hungry for her. She was hungry for it and she was glad that the feeling was mutual right now. She was going to have him for everything that it was worth. "I promise," he said with a grin on his face.

She reached out, grabbing hold of his cock and stroking the shaft as she leaned in and kissed him, her lips pressing against his and within seconds, his lips parted and their tongues met again, familiar lovers, hungry and longing for each other. Their tongues didn't lie and they didn't hide their feelings for one another. She knew that they belonged together and that they were unavoidable.

They were dancing on the edge of the abyss, but there was nowhere that she would rather be. She squeezed and stroked his cock, running her thumb over his head and coating it with the gift from the tip of his penis. He smiled as he became stiffer and harder, his cock hungrily, greedily begging for more. She gave him a tug and smiled as his body twitched. She knew that she had complete command of him and that her will was law here.

"I want you to lick me," she said, giving him his marching orders. He looked at her and he grinned, his smile a perfect picture of white teeth and alluring lips.

He was everything that a woman could ask for and she hated that she wanted everything from him. Why did he have to be a married man? Why did he have to be so powerful where there were eyes always on him? How much happier would they have been alone together in the middle of nowhere, loving each other and making love?

"You're a dirty girl," he said teasing her, his hands running over her cloth clad pussy. She moaned as he pressed against her clit, teasing her and giving her a warning of the pleasure that was about to take over her body. She gave him a soft squeeze and reminded him of who was in charge here.

"You know that's what I like," she said with a grin that was wicked and delightful. She loved oral. She loved it when she first felt a tongue running down her slit and playing with her clit. She loved it when she felt a tongue against the lips of her pussy, the warm hot breath, and the sensation of a tongue trying to cross the threshold of her pussy. It was a powerful sensation and it was one that she had been craving her entire life. She wanted it more and more after Grayson so wonderfully demonstrated how it was supposed to work.

"I'll give you everything you ever dreamed of," Grayson promised her as he dropped down onto his knees and kissed the cloth that was covering her pussy. She knew that he worshipped her pussy and that there was nothing that he wouldn't do for it. She knew that he was hungry for her and that her pussy had mesmerized him. Her body had bewitched him, but he told her that they were such a perfect fit and that he felt more alive inside of her than at any other point in his life.

Hooking his thumbs on the waist of her underwear and pulling them down slowly, he revealed her immaculately cared for pussy. She could feel the heat of his warm breath washing over her and she moaned as he leaned in and pressed his lips against her lips, sending a cold shiver down her spine. She ran her fingers through his hair and dug in deep, pushing him closer to her pussy and giving him no escape. She closed her eyes and felt her breathing pick up its pace and her heart began to pound faster and faster. She moaned, feeling his tongue running down her slit, brushing against the doorway of her pussy and then back up to her clit where he worked like a mad scientist, bringing life inside of her.

"Oh yes," she moaned, not afraid of making the noise as she held him close to her. She moaned as she felt herself getting more and more wet with each time that his tongue flicked and teased her clit. She could feel the jolts of lust shooting through her, like mad bolts of love and hunger, ripping through her as she moaned and closed her eyes. She reached up and ran her fingers through her hair and knew that it wouldn't be long for him.

He was too good. He was too talented. It was like his tongue could read her and anticipate every move and every desire that she had. But as he applied pressure to her clit, licking again and again, rubbing her and welling up the sensation deep inside of her, he began to slow down as she approached the brink.

A smile spread across her lips. "You bastard," she laughed as he slowed down and she felt her whole body begin to step back from the edge of her orgasm. She took the time to try and steady her heartbeat and to catch her breath the best as she could. She was soaking wet and as he looked up at her, laughing, she gave him a shove down on the floor and straddled his face before he could figure out what was going to happen. He clamped his hands down on her thighs and his tongue found its rhythm again and her body was revved up again alike an engine.

She moaned and rocked her hips, humping his face as she dragged her pussy back and forth over his tongue as he worked feverishly and it wasn't long before she was leaning back, running her hands through her hair and moaning at the top of her lungs. She arched her back and was screaming in pleasure, moaning and begging for him to keep doing it, to keep licking her for all that he could.

She wanted him deep inside of her and as she screamed at the top of her lungs, it felt like there was a white light swelling inside of her and engulfing her completely. There was no escaping it and the orgasm hit her, rushing over her and pulsing all throughout her body as the electric dance of lust shot through every cell in her body. It was the most powerful feeling in the world and she quickly pushed back from his face, not letting him continue to lick her. Each time he touched her, it felt like a nuclear explosion going off on her body and she couldn't handle it. She couldn't take it anymore.

"Stop, stop, stop!" she laughed, sliding down onto his chest and looking down at his eager and playful expression. He would lick her until she went insane from all the pleasure and being overloaded if she let him and sometimes she thought about letting him do it. It would be a great way to die. "God, you're talented," she reminded him.

"So long as you like it," he said with a grin.

She knew that she was soaked, but she wanted to give him a little pleasure too before she took more and more from him and she was planning to take everything that he had to offer her. There was no escaping for him. He was going to give her everything that she ever wanted and he was going to prove that he wasn't using her as some kind of sex slave to alleviate all the frustrations that he was having at home.

No, he was going to prove once and for all that he loved her and that they were meant to be together. When she looked at him, she reached around behind her and felt his rock hard cock. But before all that, she was going to give him a kiss and a lick or two.

Throwing her leg over his chest, she leaned down and she kissed the head of his cock, feeling it twitch and its unnatural warmth as she parted her lips and ran her tongue over the head of his cock, circling it and feeling it along her tongue, so soft, so strong. It was the most incredible cock that she had ever experienced.

It was like it had magical powers and that it could speak to her. All she wanted to do was to enjoy that cock and have it for herself. There was nothing more powerful than it inside of her. She took it in her mouth, wrapping her lips around the shaft and soaking it, clicking and taking it deeper and deeper inside of her mouth. She loved the heat of it against her tongue and the warmth of it that it filled her mouth. He moaned and closed his eyes, running one hand through her hair and another hand through his hair as he felt the sensation of her mouth taking him in.

She never became exceptionally good at giving out blowjobs, but she knew that if she wanted oral, that she better be willing to give them a whirl as well, but when it came to Grayson, she felt something new. She actually wanted to give him a blowjob and she wanted to drive him wild. She loved the feeling of his cock inside of her mouth and as she ran her hands over his shaft, stroking him and licking him, she liked the feeling of it. It made her even wetter and even hornier than she had been. God, she wanted him more and more with each time she felt the tip of his cock pressing against the back of her throat.

Pulling back, she caught her breath and looked at him, smiling and feeling the lust taking hold of her, possessing her in a way that she couldn't explain. "Do you like that?" she asked him.

"I think you already know the answer to that," he laughed, staring at her, wide eyed and full of his own possessive lust. There was no escaping what was coming next and it was all by her design this time. She stroked his cock, keeping him hard and eager for her, hungry for what it was that she could give him.

As she straddled him again, hovering over his long, rigid cock, she smiled at him, teasing him as she lingered where she was. She could see in his eyes that he was desperate and that he wanted her. He wanted her to come down on top of him.

And so she did, but she did so slowly, guiding his cock into her as she slipped lower and lower onto him, taking his head inside of her and feeling it as it pushed in deeper and deeper, taking all of her and she smiled, grinning as she bit her bottom lip and felt like her whole body was expanding, taking a deep breath and inhaling him as she slowly lowered herself onto him. It felt like an eternity before she felt the last of him push deeper and deeper inside of her. She was almost sitting on him, smiling at him as she thought about just how deep inside of her he was and how hot that made her, how horny she was and how aroused she could be by the thought of having a man inside of her. She wanted him inside of her all the time. It was like she was missing a part of her soul and this was finally what she needed. This was finally everything that she wanted. With him, she felt complete.

She rocked her hips and rotated, pulling his long, hard cock this way and then that way, taking him for a ride that was blowing his mind. She could see him struggling with the sanity of it all, fighting to keep his mind as she rotated her hips, rocking and making him feel like he was in a maelstrom of sexual pleasure.

But inevitably, she felt the familiar pressure building inside of her, like a boiler that was about to explode and ravage her body with delight and pleasure. As she closed her eyes and leaned back, planting her hands on his thighs and bracing herself as she worked his cock over, moving up and down and feeling it squeeze against her, thrusting in and out as she commanded it. It felt glorious to be in charge. She loved being on top, because she felt so powerful. It was the kind of experience that she relished.

He was moaning and his eyes were pinched shut as the rhythm began to pick up and it began to get more ferocious. She leaned forward, her hair dangling down over him as her breasts bounced and her breathing turned to moans as she exhaled. She was screaming as she took him harder and faster, driving him up and into her with the kind of ferocity and speed that she hungered for, that she was so desperate for.

She wanted him so badly that she could hardly contain it. There was no escaping this. She knew that in a matter of seconds, she was going to be unleashing everything she had and as he drove up and into her, harder and harder, she felt the light swelling inside of her.

He came inside of her just before she hit her orgasm and she continued to ride him, feeling his stiffening body twitch as his mouth was open in a scream of pleasure and lust, his eyes wide as he took her in, seeing her as the beautiful, heavenly creature that she was to him. She felt his whole body shuddering as the orgasm washed over her, pulsating through her and vibrating in her bones.

It was a powerful experience and as she ground her hips against him, savoring the sensation of his cock inside of her, she leaned in and kissed him. It was a desperate kiss that they shared, both of them refusing to let the moment end as the orgasm was still rippling through her, causing her skin to prickle and her whole body to feel warm, like her cells were humming in glee.

As she kissed him, she realized that this was the experience that she needed to have for the rest of her life. The anxiety and the terror that she had experienced earlier was gone, for the moment. She looked at him, kissing him as they lay together naked on the floor of her apartment. She loved the sight of him and she knew that there was nothing more in the world that she could ever want. She was never going to get over him and she was never going to move on. This was the man that she was destined to be with for the rest of her life.

Tara rolled over onto her back and laid in the pale, haunting light of the television's glow and looked at him, his face a mixture of deep shadows and pale blue light that kissed him. It was the kind of face that was both breathtaking and mysterious at the same time. When she looked at him, she knew that there was something inside of him that wanted her as much as she wanted him. He wouldn't have tolerated the torn clothes and he wouldn't have been happy with the destruction that she had caused. Harriet might see the damaged clothes, she might notice that he was gone longer than he had intended to be. But in the end, he was here and she was at the party. This was the distinct difference that she needed to know. She needed to see this.

"I want you," she told him in a way that transcended the physical nature of their relationship. "I want your time and your smiles. I want your laughter and your best moments. I want your sad days and your worries. I want all of you, Grayson."

The confession was quiet, lurking between the two of them and she looked at Grayson, reading the expression on his face. It was a distant kind of feeling inside of her, the kind of feeling that made her feel weak and vulnerable, like she was standing naked in front of him. She didn't like it. She hated this feeling, but the silence made it worse. Did he not feel this way? Was he thinking something else? Was she just blindly falling for him with no hope now? She stared at him, looking for any kind of an answer.

"I want everything from you too," he whispered softly. "I want to share you with the world and I want everyone to know that the only reason I feel like getting up in the morning is because I have you in my life. I want people to know that you are the light of my life. I want people to know that you're my heart and soul, Tara. I mean every word of what I said to you. I'm going to make you my wife and we're going to be together forever. I swear it."

She touched his cheek with her fingertips and smiled at him. She wanted to believe him. She wanted to believe him so very badly, but there was a voice deep inside of her that warned her against feeling so happy and so blissful. She needed to protect herself and she needed to be mindful of her own safety here. In the end, she didn't care.

She wanted him and she wanted to be happy forever with him. She leaned in and kissed him, praying that the cynicism would burn away and she would have the future she desperately wanted with the man that she completely and totally loved. When his lips eagerly kissed her back, she couldn't help but give in to hope.

CHAPTER SIX

She looked at him, watching him as he pulled on his clothes with the least amount of enthusiasm that she'd ever seen. There was something about Grayson right now that screamed his disinterest in going back to the party and back to his wife. He seemed like he was trying his hardest not to actually go back there and she kind of understood the draw for him to linger.

This was New Year's Eve and you wanted to spend that time with the people that you loved most in the world, not going back to the people that you hated and that you knew wanted you gone. There was nothing happy about that. So, she understood the lethargy, but this wasn't something that they could escape. This wasn't something that he could just hide from and hope that it would go away. He needed to go back.

"Are you going back to the club?" Tara asked him, feeling like she already knew the answer.

"Yeah, I've got about forty-five minutes until Harriet will actually be looking for me," he gave her an awkward smile. "I'm sorry that I'm putting you through this. I know that it's terrible. But please remember that one day it won't be like this. One day, we're going to be together."

"I know," she said. She didn't want him to leave, but she knew that it was necessary. She was going to try her hardest not to make it personal and she was going to try her hardest not to make it about her, either. She didn't want this to end on a sour note. She had just had the time of her life and she was thrilled that he cared about her enough to do this with her, so she wasn't going to feel bad for herself. There would be other times ahead. There would be more times for the dark thoughts and the grim clouds overhead. Not right now though.

She helped him, buttoning his vest as he worked on his bowtie. He was such a handsome man and his ruined shirt was going to be noticed almost immediately. She was sure that there would be someone at the club willing to give him another so that he was free and safe from the scrutiny of Harriet.

There was no way that he was going into the lion's den without it. She would see him and she would rip him apart the moment that she saw that he had a shirt that was ripped open. There was nothing more stupid than messing around with Harriet, that much she knew right now and that she wasn't going to even try to dabble with. It was always going to be better to just play it safe.

"I wish you could stay," she said honestly. She didn't want to try and guilt him into staying. No, she just wanted him to know. She thought that it was important that he be aware of the fact that she was genuinely and truly going to miss him and that there was nothing that was going to be more devastating to her than watching him go. She wanted to have him all to herself and losing him was going to be hard.

Worst of all, when she closed her eyes at midnight, she was going to know that he was going to be with Harriet and that his lips would be pressed against hers so that all the watching eyes would see that they were happily into each other and that their marriage wasn't the sham and the lie that he was professing.

"I wish I could too," he said, kissing her before he turned away and slipped on his black and white shoes. He was so handsome, so suave looking. There were very few people in the world that could pull of a white suit, but he was definitely one of them. "I want to see you again," he told her. "I want to see you soon."

"You know my number," she reminded him, kissing him softly on the lips before he turned and stepped out in the hallway. He smiled at her, smitten by her kiss and her presence. "I'm crazy about you."

"I'm crazy about you too," he whispered honestly.

When the door closed and she was shut behind it, all she could do is think about how much that she was going to miss him. She looked at the buttons strewn across the false wooden floor of her apartment, thinking about how he was truly taking a risk with her and she wondered if Harriet was going to care.

If they were unhappy, then there was no way that Harriet was alone and that she was taking care of herself. She had to have something going on the side. There was something suspicious about all of this and if Harriet was just miserable and didn't care about relationships in general, there was something wicked about her. Everyone wanted to have someone and if you didn't and all you cared about was power, then that meant you were a particularly strange person and that was scary.

Alone in the apartment, she looked at the television and knew that she was spending this year alone again and that there would be no one to press their soft lips to hers and celebrate the fact that they had endured yet another year and were excited for the promise of another year.

All of it was lost on her and as she looked at the television, she decided that it wasn't worth it to stick around and feel sorry for herself. She might as well go to sleep. At least then, all the worry and all the fear would be flushed down the tubes of her mind and into the dream realm.

But that was all held back by the fact that she felt extremely nervous. It was the kind of nervous that was hard to explain and the more that she thought about it, the more that she wondered where it was coming from. For months, she had been sleeping with Grayson and stealing action with him on the side, but never had she actually felt all that worried about it.

Tonight, however, she felt nervous for some reason. Something was wrong and she couldn't put her finger on it. She really wished that she could, that she could take it all away, but there was nothing she could do for it. She could feel the worry inside of her mind, slithering around, making her nervous.

What was wrong with her? She'd felt off for days. Sure, it might be something coming on, but rarely had anything hit her like this, so slowly without really starting to manifest itself. Honestly, she thought that she was starting to get an ulcer from the worry and the panic that she was suffering form.

She figured that there was something wrong with her, like she was getting panic attacks or she was getting anxiety from all of this. Since there were no physical manifestations of something being wrong with her, maybe it was all just inside of her head. God, she really hoped that it was all just in her head. Maybe a good night's sleep was going to be enough to get rid of whatever it was.

She walked back to her bedroom and looked in the mirror, staring at herself and wondering what she was going to do now. She took a moment and stared at herself, gazing at the young woman before her who was terrified, too afraid to do anything about what was wrong with her life. It wasn't like she could. All she could do was stare at herself and wonder how she'd gotten into this mess. In the end, all that mattered was that there was hope on the horizon. Maybe that would be enough. Maybe that would be everything that she needed.

Something inside of her roiled and spun, whirling and making her feel dizzy. There was something definitely wrong with her and as she rushed to the bathroom, she flipped up the toilet seat and clutched the porcelain bowl of the toilet and stared at the clear waters, rippling softly as she stared down into the plumbing.

She was certain that she was going to throw up. She could feel the bile in the back of her throat. It had to be whatever it was that she had eaten today. Today was the worst of the feelings. It had been so powerful that she had actually had to leave work. What was it that could have done this to her?

The nausea hit her and then rolled away, bubbling into the distance of her mind and her skin began to feel cold, like she was going into shock. There was something wrong, but she didn't know what it was. Right now, she just felt like she'd gotten away scot-free from whatever it was that had almost hit her.

She hated throwing up and she hated feeling this way worse than anything in her mind. Leaning against the wall and trying to steady her pounding heartbeat, all she could do was tell herself that it was going to be okay, that everything was fine. She was all right and she was completely fine. There was no need to freak out and there was no need to panic. All she had to do was take a moment and let herself catch her breath. She would be fine in a few minutes.

But she wouldn't be.

The thought crept into her head like a spider lurking in the shadows, coming out in to the light, more hideous and terrifying than anything else that she'd ever thought or that she'd ever seen. This was the face of true terror and the face of true fear. As she thought about it, she felt it deep in her mind. She knew that there was something wrong. There was something definitely wrong and that there was no escaping it, no making excuses, and there was no hiding it. She was going to need to face the music and she was going to need to get the answers that were going to settle the tumultuous waters in the depth of her mind.

She was pregnant.

How was this possible? She thought about it for a moment and she realized that there was no escaping the crucial reality. Her mind was connecting the dots, putting the pieces together, and the whole puzzle was fitting together once and for all. Sure, there was a chance that this was going to be a lie and this was going to be the spoof on her own fear and her own paranoia.

It was something that could totally be a lie, but she knew that there was a chance that it was going to be true. No, it was more than a chance, it was quite possibly the truth. Right now, she was rolling around the number of eighty percent in her head right now. This seemed like something that was going to come of this.

"Oh God," she whispered, looking at her stomach and wondered if she actually was pregnant, then how far along was she? How long had she been pregnant? She wasn't going to like this. She wasn't cut out to be a mother or a parent of anything. She didn't even have a houseplant.

She was too irresponsible. Heck, the man who was the father of this child wasn't even interested in having her right now. She was going to be the person who would carry the majority of this burden alone. Sure, he might give her some money to help care for the child, but there was nothing that she was going to expect from him. She was alone right now.

There was no way that she could give this child up. This was her mistake and there was no way that she could take that out on a child. She would have to take care of this child or she would suffer the burden and the horror of leaving this child for the rest of her life. She couldn't do that. She would have to grow up and she would have to take the steps to make her a parent.

Taking a deep breath, she realized that she was probably getting ahead of herself. First of all, she needed to figure out if there was something actually happening here. She needed to get a pregnancy test. She needed to find out if there was anything to get worried or worked up about in the first place. As she took a deep breath and looked at the opposite wall, she knew that she needed answers. She needed answers to questions that were burning in her mind and that was what she needed to have answers to these questions before she could figure out a plan.

Getting dressed as quickly as she could, she pulled on her coat and knew that there was a grocery store two blocks down that would have the pregnancy tests. They would have everything that they were going need for her to get the answers she wanted. She had to get her head in the right place and that was going to be her Mecca right now.

As she walked out of her apartment, locking the door, she knew that the party down the hall was in full swing and it was going to be at the apex of the celebration in about half an hour. That was it. They were all swept up in everything that was happening, oblivious to the woman standing at the end of the hall.

Making her way to the grocery store, there was nothing that could lift her out of the mental state that she was in. She didn't care about the shouting drunkards celebrating with their packs of friends or the other lonely souls out there with their hands shoved in their pockets and their heads turned down, trying their hardest to survive what it was that was looming over all of their heads.

A new year was coming and Tara was more terrified of this year than anyone else. God, what if she truly was pregnant? What if she was pregnant and she was going to have to raise this child on her own? She was going to have to leave. She was going to have to run away from New York City just so she could afford to raise this child.

But then there were the other questions that would be coming and not from the dark recesses of her mind. No, these were going to be the questions that would be coming from the pack. They were going to want to know just about every question that they could have answered nailed down with a definitive response that had absolutely no bullshit. They were going to want to know who the father was and if he was a Shifter or if he was a human. They were going to want to know where she intended to go if she wanted to leave the pack. If you just ran away, you were likely to be chased and followed, hounded and hunted to the edge of sanity. She looked at the future of those questions and cringed.

Inside the store, she tried her hardest not to freak out in front of the pregnancy tests. They were right next to the condoms and the lubes, but there was nothing subtle about that. *Want to have fun? Oops, you screwed up, better find out if it's legit.*

She cringed at the reality of her situation and walked up to the counter, grabbing a Yoohoo on her way, along with a Hershey's bar that made everything seem like she was trying to cover up what was really happening. When she looked at the clerk, he stared at the two boxes of pregnancy tests and then looked up at her.

"Having a good night?" He asked her in a dull, monotone voice. She knew that he was probably begging God to have a woman like her and here he was making fun of her.

"Peachy," she growled and swiped her card and took the bag from him. Before she left the store, she grabbed her Yoohoo and opened it up. Taking a drink out of it, she walked out into the cold, frigid air of the transitioning night. There was going to be something that ended all of this terror and this dilemma when she got home and she wanted to start the New Year knowing whether or not she was a really pregnant.

In the end, there was nothing she wanted to do right now more than just enjoy her Yoohoo and walk home and enjoy the end of the year.

But it wasn't going to be that easy.

"It's Tara, right?" The voice caught her off guard and she looked up to see the last person that she was expecting in the world standing in front of her. She looked up and she saw the woman in front of her who looked like an angel that had come down and was toying with her. "Tara Newhart? Isn't that your name?"

Tara looked at Harriet Wilkes and knew that there was absolutely no one that she didn't want to see other than Harriet. She was so beautiful and so flawless, but there was nothing that had ever looked this beautiful before. Harriet was standing in a white coat that was long, warm, and strangely perfect fitting to her. She looked at Tara with her piercing gaze.

"Mrs. Wilkes?" Tara asked nervously, looking at Harriet.

"I'm glad I have the chance to actually speak to you finally," Harriet said, stepping forward and stretching out a gloved hand that looked far more menacing that it was probably meant to be and held it out for Tara to take. She nervously shook the woman's hand. It was strong and slender. "I was hoping that I would get a chance to talk to you tonight at the club, but I was told that you were nowhere to be seen."

"How did you find me here?" Tara asked very nervously.

"We spotted you when we were driving to where you live," Harriet said and that was enough to make Tara want to scream in horror. She was just minutes away from catching her on the floor of the bathroom or even worse, straddling her husband in her living room. "I've heard a great deal about you. There are a lot of Shifters in the pack that have been whispering about you. I was glad that I was given a chance to finally meet you. I can see that the rumors weren't just errant whispers. You're truly something breathtaking to behold."

Tara was horrified about what this could be. She knew that there was something darker working in the back of Harriet's mind that scared her. What was she doing here? What was her purpose? She had to know about the affair and she had to know that there was something happening here that she didn't want to be a part of.

"Shouldn't you be at the party, Mrs. Harriet?" she asked her nervously.

"I'm not sure, I think my husband caught something," Harriet shrugged and waved off the notion. "I tried looking for him, but I think he took off. I'm not sure what I'm going to do with myself for the rest of the night. So, I thought I'd meet the girl in the pack that was making such a fuss about. I can't help but feel like I've been given a golden opportunity right now."

Her eyes darted down to the bag in her hand and suddenly there was a petrifying sensation in the heart of Tara's mind, exploding and setting off a chain reaction that ripped through everything inside of her. It was obvious that there was no chance that they were going to be able to walk away from this moment. She was looking right at the plastic bag and she could see the pregnancy tests.

She could see that there was something in front of her that was suspicious. Everything about her situation was horrifying and there was nothing that she could do to hide it. Sure, she couldn't make her look away and there was no way that she could hide the bag right now. She couldn't just hold it behind her back, but she certainly wasn't going to acknowledge it.

When she looked up at Tara, there was something inside of Harriet's eyes that was filled with fire. There was no doubt in her mind right now that there was a truth out in the open that both of them were totally aware of. There was no hiding from everything that the packages implied and Harriet had picked up on it. Her eyes were livid with a dark fire that was malicious and spiteful. There was absolutely no escaping the wrath that was boiling up inside of her. God, this was going to be horrible and she was alone.

All she could think about was how horrified she was for Grayson. He was going to be the one who suffered the most from this and she was going to set him up for the fire that was coming from her right now. It was coming for her and it was just a matter of seconds before Harriet could no longer contain the wrath.

"My husband owns the Gilded Globe, are you aware of that?" Harriet asked Tara, obviously going for some different route, some wicked flanking maneuver that was going to hamstring her or hang her. She was coming for her and there was nothing that she could do to hide from it.

"I am," Tara said. "Your husband and his parents own everywhere that I'm aware of, at least places that Shifters are welcome."

"They are very powerful indeed," Harriet said to her with a dark tone in her voice that was implying that they were not alone in being the powerful people here. She knew that there was something that she wasn't saying and that made Tara even more terrifying than before. "I've had a few suspicions as of late that my husband may not be happy with our marriage and that he might be looking for a relationship elsewhere, something new and dangerous. I wouldn't think that he was the kind of person that was going to be unfaithful to a wife, just like me.

I mean, as far as I'm aware, I'm the envy of every man who isn't envious of you, that is. But imagine my surprise that when I saw you tonight that I figured that you were going to be the one that was going to catch my husband's eye. Just for a second, the flash of an instant. Did you notice him looking at you?"

"No," she said nervously. It was a lie, but she wasn't about to admit it. She wasn't going to give her that. She wasn't going to be intimidated like this. She knew that all she wanted to do in the world right now was to run away and to never look back, but she wasn't going to give her the satisfaction of that. She wasn't going to do anything close to that.

"Well, imagine my surprise when I find out that you were gone at the exact same moment that my husband was gone," she said, stalking around Tara like she was some kind of lioness and Tara was nothing more than a wounded gazelle on the Serengeti, waiting to be killed mercifully.

"I can't help but think that my husband might be having an affair with you, Tara Newhart. If he is having an affair with you, he'll rue the day that he ever touched you. I hope it was worth it, because you're going to wish that you'd never been born when I'm through with you. You're going to be nothing more than an outcast whore, turning tricks for other worthless packs to have someone watching your back. That is, if you ever get off it."

"I'm not afraid of you," Tara lied, but she was trying her hardest to have something in her back that was more powerful and that was more enduring than anything else that she'd ever had. She didn't want to be a coward and she didn't want to be seen as weak. She wanted to be seen as tough and she wanted to be seen as a fighter. She wasn't going down like this.

"I sincerely doubt that," Harriet growled. "I suggest you get home as quickly as possible and make sure that you're not pregnant with my husband's bastard. But, if you have the great misfortune of being that unlucky, then I suggest that you pack everything that you have and I suggest that you run as fast as you can for the hills and never look back.

There's nothing for you back here and there's nothing that's going to save you. You're lost and you're completely forgotten. There will be no future of you here beyond pain and sorrow." Harriet turned and started walking toward the town car where one of the tall, hulking Shifters from the VIP lounge was standing with his arms folded in front of him. He opened the door for Harriet as she approached and let her sit down. Before he shut the door, Harriet turned and looked at Tara with a wicked grin on her face. "Happy New Year, Tara," she snarled.

Tara watched her leave, watching the car pull out into the light traffic and vanishing into the chaos and the confusion of New York City. There was nothing here to help her, nothing to support her. She thought about what it was that she was going to do and all of her options looked truly horrible. They all looked frightening to her right now. There was no escaping this and there was no running and hiding right now. She was alone in a city that was going to want her dead.

The more she thought about it, the more she figured that it would be smarter to just go to the ATM, withdraw as much as she could and buy a plane ticket to the West Coast. She knew that the Wilkes had connections on the West Coast, but at least it would put a continent between her and Harriet.

Until Grayson found a way to get rid of that woman, there was nowhere on this planet that was going to be safe for her. She needed to run and she needed to do it right now. She needed to go as fast as she could and she needed to get out of here. But she needed help to do that.

Even if that pregnancy test came back negative and she was fine, there was still the fact that Harriet knew that something was up and she was barking up the right tree. She knew that Tara and Grayson had some sort of connection and that was going to get them both in trouble. How was she going to communicate with him? How was she going to warn him? She had no idea what she was going to be able to do to help him. How was she supposed to help Grayson when she had no idea how she was going to help herself?

Either way, no matter what she did, she needed to find out if she was pregnant or not. If she was pregnant, then she was going to need to make a plan of attack to get out of the city and to relocate somewhere. She was fine with leaving everything behind, but she was going to need some obscure town to hide out in. She needed somewhere safe to hide.

The idea of safety was fleeting when she thought about just how much power Harriet was going to have at her disposal to track her down.

Throwing open the door to her apartment, she half-expected there to be a man waiting for her, lurking in the shadows of her apartment with a gun, here to kill her for the crime that she had committed against Harriet. It was such a medieval society that she was living in and that she was going to have to answer to for that and it horrified her to think that it wasn't a farfetched idea to expect someone in here waiting to kill her.

The thumping party beyond the walls of her apartment masked any kind of noise and she couldn't help but think that if she was shot right now, would anyone even notice that she was dead? Would anyone hear it? She slowly took a deep breath and looked into the darkness, pierced only by the light of the doorway.

Reaching out, she flicked on the lights, illuminating the kitchenette and living room that was her home. There was no sign of anyone that she could see right now, but that didn't mean that she was safe. There was still the bathroom, the storage closet, and the bedroom that someone could be hiding in.

As she closed the door behind her, she debated whether she wanted to lock the door or not. There was no knowing what could happen to her if she locked the door and had to run away, but what if someone was following her? What if someone was waiting to spring on the door, kick it open and murder her with her back turned?

She decided that locking it was the safer call and she nervously walked into the kitchen and grabbed a knife from her knife block, holding it ready to kill anyone that dared to be hiding in the depths of her apartment.

"Is anyone there?" she called out to the shadows and the silent rooms. "If you're in here, I'm going to hurt you if I find you. I know very important people who aren't going to like you scaring me."

There was no answer.

She didn't know what she was expecting. She had a knife and they probably had a gun or something else that was just as terrifying. If they were here to kill her, they weren't going to walk out because she had threatened them. Taking a deep breath, she walked toward the storage closet and threw it open, looking at the food that she had stuffed in there and the other junk that she was holding out hope that one day she would use in a larger apartment. Closing the door, she went into the bathroom and turned on the lights. She never had the shower curtain closed and thankfully, it was a quick sweep to make sure that everything was safe for her.

She flicked on the light to her bedroom and nervously checked the closet first and then stared into the darkness that was lurking under her bed, making sure that there was no one waiting to stab her or strangle her whenever she did end up going to sleep.

When she was confident that she was alone and that there was no one in her apartment, she hurried back to the front door and finished locking the other two locks before she walked into the kitchen and sheathed her knife. There was nothing left for her to do but to finish the deed. Taking a deep breath, she walked toward the bag, scooped up her pregnancy test and headed for the bathroom.

It was a shameful thing to think that she had gotten pregnant. She was on the pill and she tried to figure out if she had ever missed it or if there was a possibility that she'd skipped a day when they had sex. She didn't even know. Sure, there was probably a possibility, but it wasn't like she wasn't on the pill. She had taken it fairly consistently and she had been mindful of it when they'd had sex, or at least she thought that she had been. It was all beginning to drive her mad as she ripped open the box and dumped the contents of the container onto the counter.

Walking back to the bathroom, she knew that there was such a thing as a false positive and that there were always chances that what she thought was a reality was actually not, but she wasn't going to depend on that. If it came back that she was pregnant, she knew that she was going to probably try to convince herself that it was a lie, but deep down inside, she knew that it was going to be the truth.

Even if she took the second test to make sure. In the end, whatever the first test said, she was going to solidify her trust inside of its answer, even if she tried convincing herself otherwise.

In the bathroom, she sat down on the toilet and took a deep breath. This was the moment of truth and she knew that there was no turning back. This was when she found out what her destiny was and that was an intimidating prospect.

She didn't want to be pregnant, but with each passing second, there was a kind of truth to it that settled in her soul. It told her that whether or not she was ready for it, this was going to happen. Why did she even need the test? While she took the test, she tried to think about when the last time she had her period was? God, this was all so confusing. If she wasn't pregnant this time, then she was going to take better care of herself. She was going to track all of this religiously. She would never again be caught off guard by it.

When she finished with the test, she flushed the toilet and washed her hands, leaving the test on the corner of the counter and wishing that she had someone here with her right then. She wanted to know right now what it said, but she knew that she was going to have to wait an agonizing twenty minutes.

She knew that it was getting close to the end of the year. People down the hallway were shouting and chanting the numbers, counting down for the New Year. She felt nervous and excited at the same time, but it couldn't be less about the New Year. All her resolutions, all of her goals, and everything that she had hoped for was shifting and getting churned under by the prospect of what was happening right now in this bathroom.

She was almost completely convinced that she was pregnant and looking at her flat stomach, the stomach that she had carved at the gym so diligently and so religiously. It was going to swell. It was going to get large and it was going to have a baby inside of it. That freaked her out that she was going to be carrying a little tiny pup inside of her. But the weight of that began to settle on her and she realized that it was so much more than just getting pregnant. This was a death sentence if anyone found out about it, especially Harriet.

She needed to play it cool and she needed to have a plan that was actually going to work for her. She knew that she needed to tell Grayson, or that she needed to get word to him somehow that she was pregnant. If everything that he had told her was true, then he was definitely going to want to know that she was having his child and that she had a plan. Whether or not he was going to be able to help her was a different matter. She was going to need to act and she was going to need to get out of town with or without any kind of aid.

The smaller the town that she vanished to the better. She wouldn't need a driver's license if she was able to walk to wherever she was working and if she laid low in someplace like a mobile home park, she might be able to work a sob story into the mix to let her stay there without any paper work. People were always willing to give beautiful women and babies a chance to start over, fresh and clean. If she could find one compassionate soul that was willing to help her, then it would be a victory.

She thought about Tina, Laura, and Greg. She had to tell them what had happened. She knew that they would keep a secret for her and that they would take care of her in any way that they could afford to help her. There was nothing that they wouldn't do for her and right now, she needed people who were more than willing to help her escape. If they could just get her out of town, that would be all that she needed; she just needed some friends.

But, the prospect of coming clean to them and telling them that she had been carrying on an affair with their pack's alpha for months now, was something that scared her and the fact that she was carrying his bastard child was even more horrifying. They were going to freak out at the thought of that and they were going to give her hell for keeping it a secret. She knew that they would whisper behind her back and that they would talk about how foolish she had been and how she undoubtedly put a bull's eye on all of their backs.

But there was no way that Harriet could make four low level members of the pack vanish because her husband had impregnated one of them. Even she didn't have that power. The strength of the pack was entirely dependent upon the numbers of those that were in the pack. She took a deep breath and knew that things would be all right.

She would move away to a small town, get a job, raise the child to think that they were no one special, and if she was lucky, they might find another pack to raise before her child had its first transformation. If they could just have the peace and the freedom to do that, then they would be just fine.

Honestly, the idea that Grayson was ever going to be able to end the old, archaic traditions of the pack was a fairytale and a dream that was never going to last. There was no way that he could change all of that. If anything, they would be lucky to get through this alive. They would be lucky to consider themselves safe at all now that Harriet knew that he was sleeping with her, or that she strongly believed that Tara was sleeping with Grayson. There was no escaping that.

Whenever Grayson thought that he would make his move, she would be waiting, and ready to open up with both barrels for him. No, they were on their own and there was nothing that she was going to be able to do to help him. He was just as screwed as she was right now.

When the celebrations had gone on into full swing and everyone in the room down the hall were done making out and fooling around with each other, the New Year was here and the time was up for Tara. She stood up and she walked over to the counter, knowing that the truth was just inches away from her. Her heart was pounding, thumping in her chest as hard as a drum and as frantic as a charge. When she flipped over the test, she looked at it and her breath lingered in her lungs. It wasn't like she needed this. She already knew.

She was, in fact, pregnant.

CHAPTER SEVEN

"Go ahead and run that by me again?" Laura said, still wearing her outfit form the party. She was a little drunk, which meant that she'd probably gotten a little frisky with one of the Shifters in the VIP lounge when she was alone and in charge of making sure that everything was set up and that everything was just fine.

Normally, Tara would want to hear all about Laura's sexual exploits, but she had called all of them over here with the explicit purpose of talking about her sex life and finding out what her next step should be. After all, right now, she was easily the most hated person on Harriet's list of enemies; Harriet just didn't know it yet.

"I've got something very important to tell you all and I don't want you to judge me too harshly," Tara said nervously as they all sat around her table, nursing the inevitable hang over that was going to be hitting all of them tomorrow. Even at this early stage, Tara was afraid to drink anything and it scared her to think of how much she had unknowingly taken before now. Was her baby in jeopardy because she had casually had a few drinks?

"You know that we wouldn't judge you," Tina said with a happy little smile on her beautiful face. She was sitting close to Greg who was already a few drinks in himself when he opened a bottle of craft beer himself and took a swig. She looked from Tara to Greg and smiled at him lovingly. Tara had that gaze for Grayson. God, it was going to suck telling them what she had gotten herself into, but there was no hiding from it.

"Yeah, Tara, tell us what's up," Greg said with a grin. He liked it when she was uncomfortable and she knew that he had this playful mentality that only extended to the point where he was protective of her. He was like an older brother to her. Sure, he could poke fun at her, but anyone else was in serious trouble if he found out about it.

"I've been having an affair with Grayson Wilkes," she said bluntly after swallowing a deep breath.

The silence hit the room like a truck running through the front of a business. It was so powerful and it was so reckless that it was likely to blow all of their minds. They looked at her, stunned and blinking for a few minutes, trying to figure out where the booze ended and where the reality of the situation picked up. She could feel all of them grappling with the reality of it.

"For a few months now, I've been sleeping with Grayson," she continued. If they were having a hard time right now, then they were going to have a really hard time with what was about to follow. "He told me about his arranged marriage and how it's this cold, loveless pact between them, and that he wanted to choose his own mate, but never had the chance. One thing led to another and we've been sneaking around together ever since. But that's not where things get interesting. I just found out tonight that I'm pregnant."

"Shit," Laura said after a moment of silence, her eyes wide and stunned. "You play for the long con, don't you?"

"Hold up, are you certain?" Greg asked her, shocked, but completely in at this point. He leaned forward and looked at her like they were conspiring to kill Caesar now. "Have you taken any tests or anything?"

"I did tonight," she said with a simple shrug. "I'm definitely pregnant."

"You know that they could be wrong," Greg told her like she hadn't already played that game of second-guessing for an hour now. Of course, the second test had pretty much confirmed what she already knew in her heart, but what her brain was desperately trying to avoid.

"That's such a guy thing to say," Tina shook her head. "Sweetheart, I'm so sorry, but I had absolutely no idea that you were seeing anyone."

"Yeah, we started to think that you might be batting for the other team," Greg joked, thankfully lightening the mood as he did so. Tara shook her head and wished that there was something that could just make her laugh all of this away, but it was more terrifying when you were in the middle of it. "Man, Grayson Wilkes himself. That man is one handsome specimen. You've got good taste."

"Thanks," Tara shook her head. "I'm sorry that I didn't tell you before, but I know how wrong this is and I know that there's nothing worse than having an affair with a married man, but I promise you, we are actually in love. Remember the toast he gave about breaking down traditions?"

"Vaguely," Tina laughed.

"Well, he wants to abolish a bunch of the old ways so that he can clear a path for us to get married to each other," Tara said, honestly hoping that this was the case. It seemed like it was never going to happen now, but she had a dream that maybe one day that she would get word that Harriet and Grayson were no more down the road. "But, now that I'm pregnant, I can't afford to stick around for him to slowly crumble the old walls. I have to act now."

"Why?" Tina asked, suspecting that there was something else at play here that she wasn't being told.

Tara took a deep breath and shook her head. "I think that Harriet knows."

"Jesus Christ," Greg shook his head, laughing at the absurdity of it all. "Well damn, Tara. You just signed your own death certificate. If Harriet knows that you're having an affair with Grayson, then she's going to kill the both of you and anyone else who had a clue about it. The woman is a psychopath."

"How do you know that she knows?" Tina pressed.

"Yeah, maybe you're just being paranoid," Laura was sounding as hopeful as Tara had been earlier today. There was no use lying to herself about it. She knew that Harriet was well aware that she was pregnant.

"I ran into her when I was buying the pregnancy test," Tara said nervously. "She said that she knew that Grayson was sleeping with someone and she thinks that it was me. She totally saw the pregnancy tests in my bag, so I know that she's fully aware that I'm under the impression that I'm pregnant."

"No, she only thinks so," Tina said, swallowing hard. Tara felt something jump inside of her as Tina stood up and started pacing, their eyes followed her as she bowed her head and put her tipsy gears spinning inside of her head, cranking out an idea that none of them wanted to disturb. No one wanted to break the concentration that she was having right now. She looked up and put a hand on Greg's shoulder. "First things first, you have to tell Grayson."

"Definitely," Greg nodded. "It takes two to tango and if he got you into this mess, then he needs to help get you out of this mess. If you're going to keep the baby, then he needs to help you out in any way that he can."

"But what about Harriet?" Laura pressed, getting to the heart of the dilemma. "If she knows that Tara might be pregnant, then we need to get her out of the city right now. Harriet will actually kill you, or worse, she'll trade you off to another pack just to get rid of you."

"We can handle Harriet and her suspicions," Tina said with absolute confidence.

"We can?" Greg lifted an eyebrow and looked at her.

"Absolutely," she said with a sinister smile on her lips. "We'll start a rumor that Greg and I have been sleeping together casually and that I thought I was pregnant. Too ashamed and scared to go to the store by myself, I sent Tara to go get the tests for me instead. She agreed, got off work early to get them for me, and I found out that I wasn't pregnant."

"I'm not sure I want people thinking I've been sleeping around with coworkers," Greg said shaking his head.

"Would you rather have Tara dead?" Laura pressed him. "Besides, Tina is crazy about you and has been crazy about you for years. The two of you being together isn't insane. I mean, look at her, Greg. Look at how fantastic she is and how lucky you would be to have a relationship with her. Jesus, look at the writing on the wall, man."

Greg stared at Tina and there was something inside of Tara that felt the swelling pride of hope that the day where they might realize how perfect they were for each other had come upon them. Too bad it wasn't under better circumstances and the threat of death.

"Okay," Greg said softly, like the curtains had parted and he'd seen the light finally and the light was very good. "We'll do it. I mean, we'll have to make it convincing, but I think that we can sell it."

"It sells itself," Laura said. "But right now, you need to tell Grayson that you're pregnant."

"I'm scared to call him," Tara said nervously. "I'd like to, but I think that Harriet is probably watching his phone and following him. If I go to meet him or if I call him, she's going to know for sure and we're screwed. She has so many lackeys."

"Fine, I'll call him," Greg said. "I'm a guy and I have the ultimate reason to call him. I'll just tell him that one of the bears left a coat at the bar and when I was cleaning up I found it, but I didn't know how to get it back to them. If his wife is listening, she'll hear that it's legit."

"But how are you going to tell him that Tara's pregnant?" Tina shook her head.

"I'll tell him that I know Tara and that she needs him to know that his wife is on to them," Greg shrugged. "Trust me, it'll work just fine. We'll set up a time or a place, or whatever we need to for you two to meet. Once you tell him, then you need to tell him that you've got to get out of here. Because if for some reason, Harriet doesn't believe that Tina had a pregnancy scare, she's going to be coming for you."

"Yeah," Tina nodded. "You've got to run. Just tell the pack that Harriet threatened you and she was wrong, but you're still too scared to be a part of the pack anymore. They'll get pissed at Harriet and they'll be sad to lose one of their own, but in the end, they're not going to grovel for any of us lower tier members to stick around."

"Do you have somewhere to go?" Laura asked nervously.

"No," Tara shook her head. "I don't have any family or anywhere that I can run to, but I figure a small town is safest."

"You'd figure wrong," Greg shook his head. "Hunters will find you. They scour small towns looking for rogues and runaways. You need to disappear into a city where there are packs and clans."

"Okay," Tara nodded. "Do any of you have some ideas?"

"I'll make a few calls," Laura volunteered. "I know a few people in Miami. You'd look wonderful on the beach and in the sun."

"Yeah you would," Greg smiled, his drunken vibe getting to him. "I'll make that call to Grayson right now and see if I can't set something up. I'll call you when I'm done."

"Me too," Laura said, standing up and heading for the door with Greg. They were all set to their various tasks and Tara felt a glimmer of hope on the horizon. It was good to have friends like this.

"And I'll stay here with you," Tina said, sitting closer to Tara and wrapping her arms around her friend. Tara smiled and leaned in, hugging Tina and tried not to notice the tears that were rolling down her cheeks. God, she was so scared, but now she felt like there was a chance that everything was going to be just fine. Everything was going to be okay in the end.

***

Greg called less than an hour after he had left and told them that he'd gotten a hold of Grayson and that everything went off perfectly. Grayson knew that there was a coat that he needed to pick up at the club and that he was going to stop by tomorrow. The club was going to be closed on New Year's Day.

It was the day where everyone was too hung over to think about partying and the following day was a work day where they were all going to have to stumble back into their jobs. New Year's Day was about recovery and relaxation to the club world. So, when he stopped by, they would be waiting for him and that was when she would tell him everything.

Greg told her that he'd chickened out about telling him and that it was more important that the words come from her in the end. She didn't think that this was a problem. After all, she was the one who was pregnant, not Greg. She should tell him.

When she finally passed out, she felt like the world was falling apart, but some of the pieces were still holding. There were people in her life that didn't want her to tip over the edge into insanity and they were going to take care of her and make sure that she was just fine. That made her feel loved and valued right then and that was what she needed. She didn't know that friends would ever come to save her in this kind of a situation, but here they were.

When the morning came, or at least, it was supposed to be morning, the world was still dark when she rose and got ready to go tell him. She dressed quickly and did her make up after she showered. She got ready in record time while Tina just slipped into something that was casual which she borrowed from Tara. She didn't mind, but when they finally ended up at the Gilded Globe, they were let in the back by Greg who was already there.

"Head up to the VIP lounge," he whispered, watching over their backs to make sure that they were alone and that they weren't being followed. "I'll tell him to meet you up there when he shows up."

She passed Laura who was smiling at her with a kind of nervous excitement that Tara didn't feel was really necessary or acceptable right then. Either way, Tina stayed with Laura and gave her a comforting pat on the back as she headed up to the VIP lounge alone. She nervously sat alone behind the velvet curtain and waited for Grayson to arrive. It was ominously quiet in the club when they were here alone.

She could hear as the doors opened and their distant voices muttering about something with Grayson. She couldn't make out the words, but she could definitely recognize his voice and his tone. God, she loved him and the sound of him made her feel more and more comfortable than she had been before.

As he headed up the stairs and across the mezzanine, she stepped out from behind the curtain. He looked at her for a moment, confused and not sure what was happening. He stopped and looked at her, glancing down to the abandoned dance floor and cautiously walked toward her.

"What's going on?" he asked her nervously.

"We need to talk," she said, hating the words as they came out of her mouth.

"Do you think it's smart for us to be meeting like this?" he hissed, his eyes darting down to the thought of others below them. She smiled and shook her head at his nervousness. He caught on and his uncomfortable shoulders slumped. "They know, don't they?"

"So does your wife," she told him as he walked with her into the VIP lounge.

"Doesn't surprise me," he said with a shrug. "She was inevitably going to find out, but I'm not surprised."

"She confronted me and threatened me," Tara told him.

"Bitch," he grumbled as he looked at her apologetically. "I'm sorry about that. She's a complete psychopath. I didn't think that she would do that, but if she's confronting you, then there's no telling what she's going to do next. I'll need to make sure that someone's watching her at all times."

"It gets worse, Grayson," she said to him, half smiling and shrugging. "I don't know, I'm kind of fond of it, but you might not be. Don't feel bad if you're not, I just want you to be honest to me."

"What's going on?" He furrowed his brow in confusion.

"I'm pregnant, Grayson," she said softly to him.

His face illuminated and there was no hiding the expression that spread across his handsome features and she felt her heart souring and fluttering at the sight of him filling with such excitement and delight that she'd never seen him with before. His eyes sparkled and the smile that spread across his lips was the kind of smile that she'd fallen in love with ages ago. As she looked at him, she knew that this was the man that she was going to spend the rest of her life loving.

"That's incredible," he cried, throwing his arms around her and pulling her close to him, hugging her tightly and letting out an overloaded and delighted sigh. But, as his excitement was in full grasp of him, he suddenly pulled back and looked at her, putting two and two together to make a clearer picture of why he was here. "She knows, doesn't she?"

"I think so," Tara said with a heavy heart. "Tina and Greg are spreading rumors that they've been sleeping together and that I was buying the test for her because she was too ashamed to go buy it herself, but I don't think it'll last if she thinks that I'm sleeping with you. It's going to only get worse when she sees that I actually am pregnant. Grayson, I have to get out of here. I have to run away."

He nodded for a moment, his gaze distant and full of thoughts that she wasn't privy to. She knew that he was thinking about something else, already hatching his own schemes and plots. He had a whole world of thoughts and plots that he had set up that were now starting to shift. She could see them changing and shifting right before her eyes. "Absolutely," he said with a thoughtful nod. "We need to get you out of here, but not for long."

He turned and looked her in the eyes and she shook her head. "If they find out that you've been having an affair with me, she'll take her pack with her when you split from her. Everything that you were working for and that you were hoping for is going to be rendered useless."

"No it won't," he said with a grin. "I just need to keep you safe for a couple months and I'll have her gone and everything will work out perfectly. More importantly, we need to get you out of here so that she doesn't try to have you killed. I wouldn't be able to live with myself if anything ended up happening to you Tara. You're the love of my life."

"So, what do you think that I should do?" she asked him nervously. "I don't know where to go. I don't have any family left and Greg says that going to a small town is too dangerous. Laura might have some leads for me, but I don't know what I'm going to do. I have nowhere to go."

"Don't worry about that," he said with a smile on his lips. He was hopeful and that was something that gave her a little more courage and a little more hope than she had previously had. The sight of him so happy and so optimistic was something that made her feel like there was actually some hope in her life. "I'm going to take care of everything, Tara. I'm going to make sure that you're safe and I'm going to make sure that we're completely happy when all of this is over. Harriet's dominion of terror is at an end. I'm going to make sure that there's nowhere left for her to go when I'm through with her."

"What about my friends?" Tara asked him. "Are they in any danger?"

"Absolutely," he chuckled. "We all are, but if the three of them stick together and lay low for a while, they'll be just fine. I'll make sure that everything is taken care of. In fact, I think that we should go down stairs and talk to them."

"What if this doesn't work out?" Tara grabbed his arm as he turned to head out of the VIP lounge. He spun and looked at her, his eyes full of doubt and confusion as to the point of the question. It was like he wasn't even able to comprehend that there was a possibility that this wasn't going to work. She loved that about him, but she knew that even the best laid plans were susceptible of being shattered. The fact that he was here with her was enough. "What if Harriet ends up destroying everything that you've worked for?"

"Simple," he shrugged. "I'll relinquish my title and I'll go into exile with you. No bloodshed, no trouble, and no hope of returning. I'll make sure that everyone who is in danger gets the same treatment and Harriet can have her shattered empire if I end up failing, but that's not going to happen, Tara."

"You'd do that?" She asked, staring at him in baffled confusion. This wasn't the man that she had met months ago. This was a man who genuinely loved her and was talking about giving up everything that he ever had to spend the rest of his life with the person that he loved. "You'd really give up everything for me?"

"I would rather spend the rest of my life with the wife I chose and the child I fathered with her than with a woman I hate," Grayson told her. "But, I'm not letting everyone we know and everyone that we care about suffer from our decisions. I'm going to make sure that it's not just us who have the life that we wanted, but everyone else is going to end up free of Harriet and the traditions that we've been bound to for far too long."

He squeezed her hand and she felt her heart pounding. God, she loved him. She loved him more than she had ever loved anyone before and the thought that she was lucky enough to have him was almost too much. She wanted to start crying, but at the same time, she wanted to rip his clothes off and ravage him right there.

"Come on," he said to her with a grin, "let's go tell your friends what to do next."

By the time they were downstairs, her friends were all eager and awaiting whatever their marching orders were. She looked at them, studying their faces as Grayson gave them the speech he'd been waiting to give to his people since he was given the thought of tearing down the old way.

They looked at him, nodding and their courage growing, as he told them what his plot was to make them all safe and to free them from the lower tier that they were stuck in, bound by the traditions of old. They nodded in encouragement, and when he told them to stick together and lay low until this had blown over, they were more than willing to do so.

"Head home and wait for me to send word to you," Grayson told them. "I'm going to contact you personally, so don't trust anyone who says they're speaking on my behalf. Understood?"

They nodded and hugged Tara before they left. She held them close and kissed them each on the cheek. They weren't going to sacrifice for her, they were going to profit from all that they had offered her. She was going to see to it that they were all safe and that they were all free of this horrible life that they were stuck with. With Grayson leading them, they were going to be fine.

When the doors closed, they were locked in the Gilded Globe, alone and she looked up at the sparkling, golden planet slowly spinning over the dance floor. She could feel Grayson's presence and she knew that there was only one thing on her mind as she turned around and looked at him.

"You know what one of the benefits of being pregnant is?" she asked him, wiggling her finger for him to come closer to her. He grinned and approached her eagerly, more than willing to find out.

"What is that?" he asked her, wrapping his arms around her, feeling the soft gray jacket that she was wearing. She wasn't wearing a bra underneath and she wasn't wearing anything under her yoga pants either. She knew that this was going to be a quick errand and that she wanted to be comfortable for the rest of the day. She didn't want to spend the entire time in jeans and squeezed into a bra.

"I can't get pregnant," she smiled at him, biting her lower lip and staring into his eyes, hoping that their child had his magnificent eyes.

"How, at a time like this, can you think about something so dirty and naughty?" he asked her playfully, running his hands over her sides and reaching up to see that she wasn't wearing a bra, feeling through his hands that the only thing under her jacket was her soft, flawless skin. "Tara, are you wearing anything under this jacket?"

She shook her head now and smiled at him, grinning. "Who knows what tomorrow is going to hold for us?" she whispered to him softly. "We should live for today and we should enjoy every moment that we've been given. Don't you think? You know, in case we never get another chance to."

"That's a grim thought," he said reaching up and grabbing the tab to her zipper and slowly giving it a tug. She smiled, feeling the jacket come loose around her and when it was all the way at the bottom, he freed the two sides of the zipper, liberating them and the cool air kissed her naked stomach and chest, her breasts still hidden by the thin cloth.

"But, I think I could take any excuse to enjoy you. You're the most magnificent woman that's ever lived, Tara. I'll gladly give you anything you want."

"You don't want to fuck me?" she raised a suspicious eyebrow.

"I always want to fuck you," he said with a strong smile on his face. He leaned in and kissed her. He tasted of mint and she loved the smell of his fresh cologne as he closed his eyes and their lips pressed against each other, dancing and marrying to one another as his hands reached up and parted her jacket, feeling her breasts. His hands were cool and she felt her nipples starting to perk up and get excited from the feel of his hands as he squeezed her breasts, massaging them as they kissed, the passion rising and the heat of the kiss building. He ran his fingers over her nipples and she felt the shiver run down her spine. She loved it when he touched her, when he experimented with her body and probed her, getting a feeling and a sensation that was just right. He was the kind of fearless explorer who knew exactly what her body needed and she loved every second of his tender care that he gave her. All the attention that she would ever want was in his fingers and he knew how to work her.

"Play with me," she breathed. "Make me forget all of the troubles."

"I live to serve," he said, kissing her neck and spinning her around.

He brought her back to his chest, her ass grinding against his hard cock and she knew that she was in his safe hands as his arms wrapped around her, holding her tightly. His hands spread out, rising up and cupping her breasts, squeezing her to him and she closed her eyes, letting all of the sensations and the urges flow through her. She loved the power of his body against hers. He slowly took his right hand and slipped it down over her naked torso, feeling her flat stomach and sending a shiver down her spine.

Yes, she wanted him to keep going. She wanted him to go deeper and deeper down below and when he slipped his fingers under her waistband, she smiled and leaned her head back against his shoulder. God, she wanted him right now. She wanted him inside of her. Everything about this moment seemed so perfect, seemed so real and so true to her. There was nothing more perfect than having him here with her.

His fingers brushed over her slit and she shivered again. His fingers were powerful, electric beings that she was begging for. She wanted this. She wanted him inside of her and as his fingers played with her clit, she began to feel her heart picking up and pounding harder and harder. This was everything that she needed.

Closing her eyes, she moaned, letting his fingers roll over her and as he slipped deeper, swirling his finger around threshold, teasing her, forcing her to feel that euphoria that was so hard to capture without him. When his fingertips pressed deeper, pushing inside of her, she moaned and slide her hands up her body, sliding on around the back of his neck and holding him there as she opened her mouth and breathed heavily. God, this was amazing.

She knew that there was one thing that she could always count on and that was the fact that Grayson knew how to work her body. He knew how to make her feel amazing and that was something that she never gave up on. She knew that she could depend upon him and as he fingered her, probing deeper and deeper inside of her, she could feel her breath escaping her lungs, fleeing into the distance, leaving her behind and not giving her a chance to catch it.

 His thumb rolled over her clit, keeping the rhythm smooth and steady, bringing the pressure and the power of the orgasm up higher and higher until she could actually feel the warmth inside of her.

"Oh God, yes," she moaned to him. "Keep doing that."

He did just as she asked him to and as his fingers rubbed her, pushing deeper inside of her while his thumb worked her clit, she reached around behind her back with her other hand and rubbed his cock, feeling it through his pants as she moaned and tried her hardest to keep in control of herself. She didn't want to surrender completely, she wanted to keep this going. She wanted to feel everything at its most powerful, at its peak. But that was easier said than done.

He grabbed her breast, squeezing it and rolling her nipple between his thumb and his forefinger. It was the greatest feeling in the world. It was the most wonderful sensation shooting through her, but she knew that she wouldn't be able to fight it for much longer. He had a control over her body that was unavoidable, that she couldn't resist. She closed her eyes and she moaned as he continued to finger her, rubbing her clit to the point of pure ecstasy.

When the orgasm hit her, it rippled out from her vagina, shooting through her body and telling her that there was no escaping this one. It pulsed and vibrated, making her moan and cry out in pure delight and euphoria. She wanted him to keep fucking her, to have her all to himself for the rest of his life. She didn't want to share him with anyone else. This was the man that she wanted all to herself. They were going to have a child together and that was all that they needed to make this official to each other.

Trying to gain control of herself, she leaned forward, gripping the stage's lip where the DJ booth was. She smiled and tried to catch her breath. Her heart was beyond coercion and it was pounding faster and harder than it had ever pounded before. It felt like it was going to shoot out of her chest, but she knew that she wanted to keep going. She wanted him to come for her and she wanted him to take her for everything that she had. She wanted him to have every last desire that was in his heart. She knew that he had desires and that she was going to be willing to fulfill anything that he wanted, just like he was willing to fulfill anything that she wanted.

She felt his hands clamping down on her hips as he walked up to her. She smiled, her ass sticking out to him and she could feel his cock against her cheeks. She smiled and closed her eyes, still not in full control of her body that was thrumming with the power of the orgasm that had just hit her. She smiled at the thought of how much she was having sex with the man that she loved. They were going to hit a record soon for everyone that she knew.

"Give me a second," she said, leaning her elbows on the edge of the stage and trying to get control of herself. "Just a second," she begged him. If he touched her, she knew that she would be right at the brink again and that she would go lunging over into another orgasm. It was too powerful, too all-consuming for her to continue at this point.

"Anything you need," he said to her softly. The sound of his belt buckle jingling and his pants unzipping made her smile. Yes, he was getting ready for her and she was more than excited to have him. She just didn't want to be crippled by a chain reaction of orgasms that wouldn't stop and right now, that was exactly what was waiting for her.

His fingers hooked under the band of her yoga pants and she felt them drag across her skin, pulling the tight fabric off of her and freeing her ass and pussy from the cloth that hid her away from him. She smiled as he pulled it down to her ankles and spread her legs, making her part them wide. She didn't dare look. She couldn't handle it. It was going to make her hot and wet again. She was already soaked and going home was going to be awkward, but she knew that looking at him was only going to make it hotter.

So she wasn't expecting it when his tongue brushed against the threshold of her pussy, his forehead pressing against her ass as he licked her, getting her all ready and excited for what was about to happen next. "Oh God, yes," she whispered, smiling as he licked her pussy, pushing his tongue past the threshold and burrowing deep into her. When he pulled the tip of his tongue out, she parted her legs and felt the warm tip of his cock pressing against her.

She moaned at the pressure, the sense of her pussy expanding to accommodate him. It was the most powerful feeling that she had ever experienced and it kept happening to her over and over again. She moaned as he drove his cock into her, his fingers digging into her hips as she opened her mouth and screamed in delight.

God, it was so hard and it was so hot, pushing deeper inside of her and making her claw at the stage to try and get some kind of grip on reality. It felt like the entire world was leaving her and that it was fading into something colorful and bright, something magnificent and potent.

She moaned as he drove his cock deep inside of her and took all of her as himself. She moaned as he pressed deeper and deeper, grinding himself up against her. She felt his hands reaching around, cupping her breasts and squeezing them. She wanted him to squeeze them harder and harder, but she also wanted him to fuck her hard, to take her to town right now.

She wanted him to unleash everything that he had inside of him and she knew that he had a lot. She knew that he had all of it inside of him, like a sports car getting ready to open up everything that he had. She pressed her ass hard against him, grinding and moaning at the feeling of his cock impaling her. Oh yes, she wanted him to go hard.

"You doing all right?" he asked her with a laugh. "Everything good, beautiful?"

"Yes," she exhaled with a thrill in her voice. It mirrored the chill that ran down her spine. "Give it to me, Grayson. I want everything you have."

"Anything you want my dear," he said with a smile in his voice that she could hear. She loved that. She loved how much he wanted to please her. Gripping her sides, he braced her, getting her ready for the heavy assault that she was needing, that she was begging for.

When he pulled his cock slowly back out of her and began to drive it back in, thrusting it deep into her, she let out an excited yelp, not expecting him to be so fast about it. He was a passionate and a kind lover. He wasn't the kind of man who would jump at the possibility and the demand of her to actually be rough about it. She was pleased that he was more than willing to accommodate her changing needs and desires, because there was something wild and feral inside of her that needed his attention right now.

He drove his cock into her, his balls slapping against her as he picked up the speed and the pace and it became a mind numbing blur to her. She couldn't tell what was happening and what was in her mind. She moaned and screamed, her back arching as she pushed her ass against him, picking up the pace that he had adopted for this and she loved every second of it. She wanted more and more of it and as he was bringing her closer and closer to orgasm, she smiled at the sensation of it. His cock ramming deep inside of her, her pussy stretching to its euphoric limits, his balls slapping against her pussy, her breasts jiggling and shaking, and the breath caught in her throat. It was everything that she ever wanted.

The spark went off in the back of her mind and she could feel it igniting deep in her pussy, exploding in that familiar wave of a chain reaction that spread through her entire body, crippling her so that every shockwave completely absorbed her body and wiped away any desire she might have to do anything else with her life. She wanted to live to fuck now and she wanted that more than anything.

The wild creature inside of her was mad and angry, it wanted more and as she moaned she could feel him reaching to her arched back and her whole body going tense and then suddenly soft with the impact of the orgasm. She smiled at his reaction to her and she wasn't afraid to stop.

"Did you go again?" he asked her in disbelief.

"Yeah," she said, pulling herself out of him and kicking off her yoga pants that were tangled around her feet. Her body felt distant, vibrating and numb as if it were in another reality that she wasn't privy to. She was completely gone, on another planet, watching her standing mostly naked and disheveled in front of the man that she was in love with. He was handsome and beautiful in the way that you would picture a god from the ancient world. It didn't seem real at all that she was here with him or that he was that good to her.

She could feel herself reaching out and forcing him onto his back in the middle of the dance floor, his cock erect and pointing straight up at the glittering, shining planet overhead. She wanted to be fucked under the globe. She wanted him inside of her as she felt everything that was humanly possible for a woman to feel like a woman. As she mounted him, she could see that he was eager to please her. He was eager to give her everything that she wanted and that was good, because she was going to demand a lot from him.

She slipped down onto his cock that slipped inside of her as easily as it was meant to, like it was going home after a long time away, wandering the world and grateful to be back with her. She smiled at how quickly it pushed inside of her and as she sat down on top of him, she felt the familiar chill as the orgasm kept pushing through her, kept flowing over her and rippling. It wasn't done and she was just getting it all excited again. She moaned and rocked her hips forward and side to side, feeling what it was like to have him inside of her. She liked the feeling. She wanted him inside of her all the time.

The great thing about being on top of a man who was perfectly made for you was the fact that you were in complete control. His cock wasn't smaller than usual, it wasn't too fat, it wasn't too long, and it wasn't weird for her. It was just right and there's a certain bliss that comes with finding the perfect cock that you were meant for.

It was the feeling of completeness and she knew that she was never going to want another inside of her and she was never going to want to feel anything remotely different from this in the world and right now, as she pulled herself up and slammed her pussy back down over the cock, she was in charge of everything that happened to it.

His fingertips gripped her breasts, squeezing them as he leaned his head back and fought the urge to blow everything right then. She could see the struggle in his eyes and she knew that he was fighting with everything that he had inside of him. That was fine, because Tara was losing her mind right now. The last orgasm never stopped and she was just making it more and more powerful, reigniting the flames with ever pump and every touch of his cock against her. She screamed in delight and moaned as she made sure that he was giving her everything that he possibly could. She wanted so much from him. She wanted everything that he could possibly give her.

"Oh God, yes," he moaned, his voice getting frantic, like he was being possessed by the spirit of lust itself. She knew that feeling. She knew it all too well. It was the feeling that swelled inside of her when she had him with her, when his tongue was licking her clit or when he was ramming his cock deep inside of her. She knew that feeling as the rapturous moment that she had to give in to everything that she ever wanted. "God! Fuck yes! Oh God!" He screamed, throwing his head back.

Tara leaned back and looked up at the luminous, glowing globe with all of its sparkles across the surface, glittering and shining on them as she felt the orgasm hitting her with brutal vengeance. Grayson's fingers dug into her sides as she moaned, screaming for him as she felt his cock ramming as deep inside of her as it would possibly go, fitting inside of her and taking her for everything that she had. She moaned and screamed at the sensation. It was so powerful that she didn't know what she was going to do if she never had him again. It would be torture.

"Oh God! Yes!" She screamed at the top of her lungs.

CHAPTER EIGHT

It felt like an eternity since she was under the globe and she was feeling the most powerful orgasm that she had ever felt before, ripping through her body and making her feel like she was the woman that she always knew that she was. It was gone, long gone and it was sad to her. She glanced over at the clock and saw that it was less than an hour, but time had changed since yesterday.

Time had become something wicked and malicious that was out to get her. There was no trusting it, because it was always lying to her. It would feel like an hour had passed, but it had only been minutes. Everything was wrong and it was starting to get to her. She felt like she was losing her mind. Was this because of the paranoia and the fear? Or was it because she was pregnant? She figured that it was probably a mix of both and shook her head. She needed to get herself under control. She needed to stop freaking out.

Ultimately, she was left with the single task of getting ready to flee the city. Grayson had told her before they left, when they were done cleaning up and making out with each other, that she needed to flee the city and that her very life was at stake. Without anything protecting her or anything that they could use against Harriet to keep her safe, she was a sitting duck and Harriet would gladly expose their weaknesses for them.

They figured that it was time to get her out of here and that they probably should have done it sooner. Of course, the fact that Harriet had blatantly told her that she knew that they were having an affair made everything feel all the more dire.

Grayson had promised to take care of the apartment, but everything inside of it that she was afraid of losing forever, it needed to be in two bags before noon and they needed to be set to go immediately. She looked around the apartment and felt like she was being forced to pick between the precious few memories that she had. She had a backpack and a piece of luggage that was supposed to fit everything that she had. It was the hardest decision of her life.

She tried to think of what it was that she was going to need right away. Grayson was going to meet her at the bus station where they were going to buy the ticket just minutes before the bus actually left. If anyone was following them, it would be best to keep them guessing all the way until the end. It was a kind of game right now and that wasn't making her feel any better, but so be it. She would do what she needed to in order to survive. So, ultimately, this was a question of essentials. What was she going to need the moment she arrived somewhere?

Grabbing as many clothes as she could, she made certain that she had most of her underwear, three pairs of jeans, skirts, a dozen tops, and five dresses. When she looked at what little space that left her in her luggage, she felt like she was going to break down and cry. She was supposed to start her entire life over with just two bags? She crammed everything else she couldn't pack in her toiletry bag into the back pack and within the hour, she was ready to get out of there and move on with her life.

Well, no, that wasn't the truth, she wanted to have so much more, but there was no time to take it all. She was in serious trouble and she needed to flee with most of her life being left behind. She had no idea what was going to happen to any of this. It could all end up in the garbage for all she knew, or it could be waiting for her on the other side of this crazy journey, but right now, she knew that there really weren't a whole lot of options available for her. She was panicking. She could feel the stress of everything coming down over her.

Wrapping her coat around her, she bundled up for the arctic weather outside in the miserable world beyond her home and she figured that it was time to start with the second part of the plan. She needed money and that meant that she was going to have to go to the bank and she was going to need to withdraw everything that she had in her checking and savings account. That was enough to make her want to cry also.

She had been working so hard to build up a life that was respectable and new. She had wanted to turn over a new leaf here in New York, but things were falling apart left and right for her. There would be no better apartment or any prospects of having a better job, all of that was gone. There was nothing that she was going to have for her. She was going to blow it all going on the run and trying to get away from a psychotic woman who was trying to kill her and her unborn child.

She was feeling the weight of everything coming down around her. She didn't have the money for medical bills and she didn't have the kind of money that she was going to need to take care of herself and give birth to a child. Babies were extremely expensive and she was leaving the one stable job that she had had her entire life. She was throwing it all away to go off on some stupid adventure to restart her life, again. She shuddered as she walked to the elevator and pressed the button.

The apartment building was ominously silent today. It was like everyone was sleeping off their hangovers and their bad decisions that they had brought upon themselves. She knew the feeling all too well. She felt like she was living a hangover right now and that it was going to stick with her for a few years at the latest. She had no idea how long it was going to take Grayson to set things right again. There were so many balls in the air that it made her want to pass out from the confusion.

When she walked down the street, she was glad that it was lighter than usual and that there were fewer people bustling and shoving to get to wherever it was that they were going. But, she didn't like the reality that when she was looking at the bank, she realized that today was a national holiday. The banks were all closed.

She wasn't going to be able to close out her accounts and she wasn't going to be able to get all of her money from them. She looked at the ATM on the outside of the building, shivering against the cold and realizing that she could take it all out at three hundred increments, but that was going to charge her extra after the first transaction. God, this was a nightmare.

She walked up to the ATM and slipped her card in. It beeped for a moment and she waited for the machine to warm up or figure out what it was doing, whatever was taking so long. She checked her phone and saw that no one had emailed her, no one had messaged her, and no one had called her. There were no voicemails or texts and that was starting to scare her.

Either that was a very good thing, or that was a very bad sign. She glanced up at the ATM and saw that it was ready. She keyed in her pin and worked her way through the system, deciding that withdrawing three hundred dollars was her only decision right now. She didn't have tons of money and she couldn't afford to pay extra withdrawal fees. She would have to use her card when she got to wherever it was she would inevitably end up.

Grayson had warned her that using her card anywhere was going to be dangerous and that there was a good chance that Harriet would be able to find her. They had terrifying friends all throughout the world and the Shifter community was tight, especially when a beautiful and powerful woman demanded to know something or asked for a favor.

Everyone wanted to have a favor from Harriet Wilkes in their pocket. But, that was her only choice right now. She would take the chance and if Grayson was smart, he would have some other way to help her before the end.

The money rolled out of the machine, a thick stack of twenties, the kind of stack that she hadn't seen in a long time. She would always get her tips made out to her in checks or have them directly deposited into her account from Luke when it was time to get paid. She wasn't like Laura who always took her cash directly, the moment she left the club. She had always thought that having it stuffed into the account immediately was smarter than taking a bunch of money home.

That showed her what it meant to be smart and to take care of herself. She shook her head and stuffed the money into her purse and looked around at the street, making sure that no one was watching her and thinking that she was some suspicious and strange woman. Honestly, it felt like she was in a spy movie and that she was some kind of criminal on the run. It was terrifying and she hated every second of it.

Of course, it was better when she hadn't noticed that there was someone watching her, about a block back. She looked around, making sure that she wasn't being followed and she was just about to the point where she was about to berate herself for being paranoid when she spotted him. He was standing near a bus stop, trying his hardest not to look like he was following a young woman, but it was painfully obvious that he was following her and that he was watching her. She looked at him for a moment and then realized that she was in danger.

She was not nearly as safe as she thought she was, and she was about to get caught. She was about to get snatched up and there was nothing she could do. She didn't know how to fight, she didn't know how to protect herself. It wasn't like she was a trained fighter or anything. She had never needed to know anything like that.

The panic was coursing through her as she looked at the man. She tried to place him and she realized that it was the man who had showed up at the VIP lounge first and told her that she had nice legs. She looked at him and she couldn't help but feel terrified. He had an annoying haircut and he looked like the kind of man who would sniff women's shoes when they weren't looking.

He was wearing sunglasses and he was glaring at her, looking about as obvious as a purple thumb. His long wool coat made him look like he belonged in the mafia, which he was practically confirming by showing up here and following her. The sight of him was so disturbing that she didn't know what she was supposed to do right now. Was she supposed to scream and run from him?

How do you lose a man who is following you? She looked at him and watched as he looked down at his phone that he was holding in his gloved hands. She stared at him for a moment, trying to figure out what it was that he was doing until he lifted the phone to his ear and was acting like he was on a call.

Maybe he was, but she didn't understand it. If he was spotted, why was he just now trying to act all sly and hidden? But when he looked up and stared at her, she realized that he wasn't trying to remain hidden. He'd been made and he was reporting in. He was definitely asking for his marching orders.

The panic swelled in her.

If there was one, then there were bound to be more. There were probably two or three of them tracking her right now and she knew that she needed to make her actions very clear and very carefully. If she went to anyone, it would be implicating them and if she led them straight to the bus station, then they were going to see Grayson when they were supposed to meet up. She didn't know what to do and the panic was settling inside of her, stagnating and festering her whole body with the poison of it. She knew that she needed to make a decision right now. She needed to find out what it was that she was going to do.

Tina.

Tina would know what to do.

Fishing her phone out of her pocket, she looked up her friend's number and she dialed it. If there was anyone out there that was going to give her solid and useful advice, it was going to be Tina and she decided to take advantage of that right now. She felt like she was phoning a friend right now on a game show that had stakes that were a little too high for her.

"How's it going?" Tina answered.

She didn't know what Tina was doing right now, but she wished that she was here right now. Tina was probably with Greg and Laura, keeping safe from anyone who was bound to end up following them. She hated that she had been the source of all of this trouble and all of this pain. It was her fault that they were all in this situation and she had no one to blame but herself right now, but she needed to ask one last thing of her friend.

"I'm being followed," Tara said as she turned and headed the opposite direction of the man who was definitely following her.

"Are you sure?" Tina was justifiably suspicious.

"Yeah, it was the guy at the VIP lounge yesterday that warned us of the wolves coming up," Tara said, confirming any doubt and any suspicion that Tina might have.

"Did Grayson send him?" Tina asked her.

"I don't know," Tara said nervously. "I don't think that he would send someone to follow me without telling me a head of time."

"Where are you?" Tina asked her.

"I'm outside of my bank and I'm supposed to be going to the bus station right now," Tara said anxiously as all of the faces around her started to meld and change into things that were fearsome and terrifying. She didn't trust anyone. She didn't want to speak to anyone and she didn't want to have any of this be a part of her life.

She wanted to scream and run as fast as she could. As she looked over her shoulder, she could see that she was still being followed. She was being tracked by the creepy guy who was still on the phone talking to whoever it was giving him orders—probably Harriet.

"Then just go to the bus station," Tina told her sagely. "If Grayson is going to meet you at the bus station, then the two of you are going to be safest if you end up going to the bus station like you originally planned. Besides, he probably has a ton of people who are in charge of keeping the two of you safe now."

"I should call him," Tara nodded, seeing that her friend was much wiser than she ever was. "I should give him a heads up."

"Okay, do that," Tina added. "Greg, Laura, and I will be at the bus station as quickly as possible so that we can help get you on safely. We don't want anyone stopping you from getting away safely."

"Thank you so much," Tara said with a weight of relief coming off of her shoulders as she talked to her friend. "Thank you for everything, Tina."

"You're my best friend, Tara," Tina told her with a strong voice. "I would do anything for you."

"I know," Tara genuinely did feel like her friend would do anything for her. It was a good feeling to have. It reminded her that she wasn't alone.

When they hung up on each other, Tara looked at her contacts and she found something that she thought she was never going to have to use and the thought that this was going to be the first time that she ever used it scared her. She stared at the number in her contacts and felt like she was about to cross a line that was never going to be able to be uncrossed. She was going to call Grayson Wilkes. Never before had she called him.

Their meetings had always been prearranged with each other in person or a spur of the moment kind of tryst. They never called each other, they never text each other, and they did so with a strong purpose and conviction that they weren't going to get caught and that they weren't going to let anyone know that they were in love with each other.

Swallowing her fears, she pressed the button and listened as the phone dialed. She knew that he had her number and that he had probably been tempted just as much as she had been to call the number before. She had looked at the number for hours at night, contemplating whether it was smart to call him or not or whether or not she should just throw her phone away. It was hard being so secretive, but as she listened to it dial, she was eager to hear his voice. She had always been so thirsty for his presence. Her heart pounded against her chest as she waited, begging for him to answer the phone for her.

"This is Grayson Wilkes," the recording picked up and she felt terrified. Maybe he was with his wife right now and he couldn't talk. Maybe he was in the bathroom or he had to deal with something that prevented him from talking.

She didn't know that this indicated anything particularly ominous or bad right now. It just meant that he didn't have his phone with him at the moment. She listened to the recording and tried to convince herself that it wasn't something serious. Everything was going to be just fine. She took a deep breath and listened for the beep.

"Grayson, I'm on my way to the bus station," she said into the receiver of the phone anxiously. She looked over her shoulder and she could see that the lackey who was following her was still a good distance behind her, at least a block now.

"I'm being followed by one of the Shifters from the VIP lounge last night, the wolf who came and told us that you were coming up to the lounge. I don't know if you sent him, but I strongly doubt it. I think that Harriet is on to us. Call me as soon as you can, I'm scared."

When she hung up the phone, she realized just how scared she truly was. She was terrified of everything that was happening and she felt like she was about to pass out. There was no escaping Harriet, it felt like she was officially locked in Harriet's world. How was she supposed to get out of the city alone? She supposed that calling a cab might be the safest bet right now. She could hop in to the cab and they could drive until her three hundred bucks were out and then she would start over fresh.

"Looking for a ride?" a voice asked her and she looked up and found herself looking directly into the sunglasses of a man who was clearly a foot and a half taller than she was. She looked at him and his familiar crew cut and she recognized him as one of the bodyguards that had been there last night as well. He looked like he was a little paler than he had been the day before, which suggested that he was probably nursing a fierce hangover that was coming back with a vengeance for him. She stared at him, wondering if he was as weak as he looked. She thought that maybe a scream would be enough to set him off.

"Get your hands off of me," she snapped at him realizing that his hand was on her elbow. She ripped it free of his hand and turned away from him, stepping backwards and not wanting anything to do with him. She said it loud enough that he reached up and rubbed his head, massaging the pain that she had caused him and it was good to see that she wasn't entirely worthless right now.

"Look lady, I got orders to bring you in and that's how this is going to go," he said to her with a voice that sounded like he expected her to just roll over and let him sling her over his shoulder before he carried her away. "Don't make me do anything that the both of us are going to regret tomorrow."

"You don't scare me," she told him firmly.

"I don't care if you think you're brave, lady," he said adamantly. "I'm not here to be your friend or the big bad wolf. I'm just an errand boy and right now, you need to get in the car."

She watched as a black town car pulled up on the side of the road. She recognized it as well. She knew that this was the car that Harriet had been carted to and from the convenience store in. The sight of it sent a chill down her spine. She didn't want to disappear right now and she realized that she was in dangerous territory to being carted off and stuffed away in some kind of prison that Harriet had built for her. Well, that was too bad. She wasn't playing along.

Behind her, she knew that she had the familiar errand boy who had shown up to warn them that the wolves were coming to the meeting tomorrow. She knew that he was at least a block behind her and that there was nothing she could really worry about right now that concerned him. She knew this neighborhood well and she knew all the alleys and she knew all the streets like the back of her hand. There was no way that she was going to get out smarted by these people. Right now, her biggest concern was the man right in front of her, but that wasn't much of a threat because she knew that a simple scream was probably enough to send him running and gripping his head.

She also knew that there was a driver in that car waiting for her and that he was going to be the second easiest to lose, because navigating New York streets wasn't easy when you wanted to chase someone. She just needed to move quickly and throw them off her trail as quickly as she could. She knew that it was a matter of finding the right hiding spot and sticking with it.

Of course, there was no knowing if there were other lackeys out there who would be chasing her down. She needed to stop thinking and she knew that her only option here was to run and if she didn't do so quickly, then she was risking getting caught and dragged off to Harriet.

She took a step back from the man, glancing over to the alleyway nearby with a truck halfway pulled out if it. It was going to be a tight squeeze and she glanced down at the lackey's shoes. He was wearing something that was dangerously close to dress shoes. He wasn't going to be able to chase her down.

"Give Harriet my regards," Tara said to the man, growling it sinisterly before she turned and took off running.

"What the hell are you thinking?" the man shouted at her venomously. "Hey, get back here!"

She didn't listen to him. All she could think about was the running, how fast she needed to get out of there and where she was going to go the moment she was free. She was going to head to the bus station and that was what was going to put her right in the same area as Grayson, which in the end was all she needed.

If she was with him, then she knew that she was going to be safe. There would be no way that they would touch them if they had the future Alpha to contend with, even Harriet wasn't that brave. There was no way that anyone would be willing to fight against him. He was the king here and that would mean that she was safe.

She headed past the truck, listening as the man with the hangover rushed to catch up with her. She knew that he was struggling, huffing and puffing as he tried to squeeze between the truck and the alley walls. Tara didn't wait and she didn't hesitate either. She was completely safe for now. Rushing as quickly as she could, she took a sharp right and headed down another alley in between the businesses. There was a parking garage nearby. If she could make it to the garage, then she would have a chance to find safety among the cars.

There was no way that they were going to search the whole thing. It would be easy to slip past them and double back. All she needed was to be smarter than they were and she was going to be totally fine. She made her way down the alley and could tell that she was on the side of the building that was the parking garage. Above her for five stories were open except for the first floor. It was just one more turn after she got to the end of the alley and she would be able to walk right into the parking garage and hide from these psychopaths.

But, as she approached the end of the alleyway, she froze as a car sped up and came to a full stop, reckless and chaotic at the mouth of the alleyway. This wasn't the town car she saw earlier. This was another one. There were more people after her than she realized and that was a terrifying thought. The sight of it was horrifying and the more she looked at it, the more she wondered if there were people on the ground chasing her as well.

How were they going to get her without Grayson knowing? What was the plan here? The thought of how far they were willing to go was horrifying to her as she took a step back and two men jumped out of the back of the town car. They were wearing black coats as well, looking as intimidating as they possibly could. These were men who lived to make people terrified and they were the people that the wolves sent to scare the other Shifters, to protect one another.

"It's time to give up, lady," one of the men said with a loud bark of a voice, not willing to play any games with her. All she could do was stop and slowly back up from them. "We're not here to play any more games with you. It's time for you to just give up and go have a chat with the lady upstairs."

"I'm not going with you anywhere," she said to him. "Do you know who I am?"

"Yeah, you're some little girl way below her station trying her hardest to get in trouble and get herself killed by her betters," the man said with a grin. He was clearly very happy with what was happening. This was the kind of caste-like idiocy that she knew Grayson was trying to get rid of. It was hard for her to get over how ridiculous it was that they genuinely believed this. They were people who thought that they were better than her just because someone told them that they were better. "Nowhere to run," he said.

She looked behind her and she saw the man with the hangover coming around the corner behind her, trapping her. He was wheezing and panting, his face crinkled and furrowed with agony as she looked at him. There was nothing that she could do right now. She knew that she was trapped and that there was nowhere for her to go. She was going to have to find a way to escape some other way. She reached into her pocket and turned her phone on, feeling by the vibrations of her fingertips. She dialed the last number that she called. She prayed that nothing would hold up the voicemail.

"Where are you taking me?" she demanded from them. She knew that they were going to take her away, but she hoped that they would tell her something that she could pick up and deliver to Grayson. She wanted to give him something to work on to help find her.

"We're going to go have a chat with Harriet," Hangover said. "Just get in the damn car."

There were no other options. She took a step forward and started to make her way toward the car, there was no sense in fighting this. There was no point to make sure that there was more time to fight right now. Instead, she needed to be able to fight later on down the road. She was going to need the strength to oppose Harriet when she finally found her. Well, when they finally took her to the woman. She didn't want to be such a victim, but this was how it was going to work out. This was how everything was going to go now, her alone against her nemesis.

CHAPTER NINE

When they brought the car to a stop, this was not where Tara expected them to take her. In fact, this was the last thing that she least expected. Harriet was the kind of person who was much smarter than they ever gave her credit for. They always thought that she was something different, something cruel and brutish, but she was far more cunning than she had ever given the woman credit for.

That was something that she was really going to regret now. How were they going to be able to find her when this was going to be the last place that they would look? After all, when was the last time that she even came to this place without there being a meeting?

Tara looked at the Gilded Globe and she knew that this was here for a reason. There was a point to all of this and that wasn't going to be able to stop anything. They were going to be looking in the wrong spot and that was all that mattered. Harriet had won this round and there was no going back. She was going to keep Tara here as long as she needed until she decided to kill her, dismember her, or whatever horrible thought she had in mind for dealing with her. She cringed at the thought of what might happen to her next.

"Come on," the man next to her in the back of the car said. "It's time to get this over with."

"You realize what Grayson is going to do to you when he finds out what you've done to me?" She asked the man.

"You think Grayson is in charge of anything?" The man laughed. "There's nothing that he can possibly do to us. Harriet is the one who is in charge of everything. She's the one who has been pulling the strings for years now. It's time for you to finally get that, lady."

"He's going to make you outcasts," she said to him with a growl as she stepped out of the car and into the cold, January air. "It's worse than death to be without a pack and you're going to figure that out soon enough for yourself."

"Yeah, keep telling yourself that," the man grinned maliciously. "Whatever keeps you from crying more."

She wasn't going to cry, though. She knew that she was in the darkest position in her entire life and that there was very little for her to negotiate with. There was no bargaining and there was no fighting this. All she knew was that she was in trouble and that she was alone. This was her deepest and darkest fears from the moment she figured out that she was pregnant. Even when they had been sneaking around, she didn't even think that this was a possibility, but now she was in for it. This was the grand finale of everything.

The Gilded Globe was empty and it was the kind of empty stillness that made her uncomfortable and fearful all over. There was no one here except for the people that were escorting her. As she stepped in through the front doors, the men with her locked the doors. Outside, the sounds of the town car that had brought her here took off and headed for the horizon. They were going to get out of here and be long gone

155

before Grayson or anyone else ever showed up, not that they had to worry about it.

Everyone that she knew who would be able or willing to help her was at the bus station and she was at the Gilded Globe. She wondered if they would ever find her body. The men next to her led her all the way to where Luke had his office tucked away. She walked back to find that Harriet was sitting behind the desk, her feet up on it and her eyes on the phone that was in her hands.

"About time," Harriet said, leaving her feet right as they were and still looking at her phone. She didn't bother glancing up to make sure that it was Tara that they had brought her. She was too confident in them. She knew that there was nothing that was going to happen to her plan. It was all going to go off perfectly. When she finally looked up, her cold, calculating eyes ran over Tara and studied her defiant prisoner with revelry and happiness. "How's it going, Tara?" she asked with a wicked smile flicking across her lips.

"What am I doing here, Harriet?" she asked defiantly, refusing to give up anything. Harriet thought she knew everything, but there was no way that Tara was going to give her anything that might validate any of her reasonable suspicions.

"Imagine my surprise that after we have our little talk, you pack up and decide to leave," Harriet said, taking her feet off the top of the desk. She leaned forward and stared at Tara with the kind of evil eyes that Tara always knew lurked in her skull. She hated Harriet, not because of the fact that she was married to the

156

man that she wanted to be married to, but because she was the kind of elitist monster that made being a Shifter so terrible.

She thought that she could get away with anything. For once, she wanted Harriet to know what it was like to be the inferior one. "It's like you might have a guilty conscience or something to hide from me that you didn't want me to figure out. Have you got something that you need to confess to me, Tara? I'm told that I'm a very good listener."

"I doubt that anyone has ever said that about you before," Tara said boldly.

"Careful; remember who it is that you're talking to," Harriet cautioned her little prisoner who was clearly not quite as broken spirited and fearful as she had wanted. She wanted Tara to be a groveling mess who would confess to everything right at the moment that she was thrown down in front of Harriet. No, that wasn't what was going to happen at all. There was no way that she was going to give in to this monster's demands. Harriet would eat her for breakfast if she showed any signs of weakness, especially right now.

"I'm not afraid of you," Tara told her bluntly.

"Your packed bags and your attempts to run away speak to the contrary," Harriet said with eyes that were relishing this far too much for Tara's comfort. She hated that Harriet thought that this was all a game. This wasn't a game. This was life and death and she knew that she was going to have to protect herself. When someone wanted information from you, the only way that you could definitely protect yourself was if you actually kept your secrets locked away. If she wanted Tara dead, she wouldn't have brought her back here to gloat with her.

No, she would have brought her to some dock or to the middle of nowhere so that she could kill Tara and be done with her. Bringing her back here only showed that there was something that she needed from Tara. Yes, needed was the right word. This was an act of desperation. "I think you're a lot smarter than you are giving yourself credit, Tara. I think you know exactly what it is that I want from you and you were smart enough to try and get away while you could."

"I'm not playing games with you," Tara said again.

"You have committed a crime against your very pack," Harriet snapped angrily. "Don't think that you're in the position to negotiate or that you have a say in anything. You're the one who is on trial here, Tara. I'm the one who is going to get to decide your fate."

"This is criminal," Tara growled. "Even for the clandestine nature of the pack, you can't just have someone intimidated or tortured because you feel that it's necessary. There are rules and you can't threaten me."

"I can do anything that I want," she said very cold and very darkly. This was the voice of a woman who wasn't playing around and who wasn't afraid of doing a thing that was beyond the realm of right and wrong. She was the kind of dark and sinister who knew that there was no one who was going to stop her and so she would stop at nothing to get what it was that she wanted.

"No you can't," Tara said firmly. "I'm not sticking around in a pack where the beta thinks that we're just play things for her to use whenever she wants to. I won't have my life be lived in fear. No. I'm going to find another pack where I don't have to be accused of being a whore just because the Alpha looks in my direction. I'm not the idiot hayseed that you think I am, Harriet. I know that I have rights."

"And I'm not an idiot either," Harriet said to the point. "I know that you think you're something special just because all of the boys look at you and that every man who crosses your path wants to sample the goods, but I am the Beta and I am the one who gets to decide who lives and who dies. If you don't give me what I want, then I assure you that you and whatever little bastard is inside of you is going to die."

Tara smiled at the threat, her hand sitting inside of her jacket, holding the cellphone and certain that it was getting recorded on Grayson's voicemail. Even if she ended up taking drastic measures and harming Tara or killing her, there would be no escaping the kind of punishment that would come down on her afterwards. A threat of death that was unprovoked and unwarranted was something that no pack would stand, especially if it was coming from a power-hungry Beta.

"What exactly is it you want from me?" Tara asked her, tired of this game and ready to get on with whatever it was that she was waiting for. There was a reason that she was here right now and that she was being held prisoner in this kangaroo court and she wanted to hear it. She was tired of all of the theatrics and the games.

"I want a full confession of my husband's infidelity and an account of your affair," Harriet said bluntly. "I want you to sign a testimony, telling of how he had sex with you, impregnated you, and I want you to stand as a witness against him when the council is convened to sign the executive powers of an Alpha over to me. I'm going to take my husband's balls, title, and inheritance in one single sweep and you're going to be the one that hands them to me."

"Why do you think that I would ever agree to that?" Tara said, shaking her head. "I'm not even pregnant."

"A quick test will come to the truth of that," Harriet said with a wicked grin. "I'm very certain that once you're found pregnant and the accusations are presented, Grayson's aging father and mother will more than happily attempt to placate my father by trying to prove you wrong and discredit you. A DNA test is all that we'll need to see that my husband is a liar, an adulterer, and unfit to rule the pack. I'll have everything I need to depose him and put someone on the throne that is worthy of the title."

"So that's all you want?" Tara shook her head. "All you care about is getting the title to the pack's leadership? You don't actually care about whether or not your husband actually cheated on you, you just want to get rid of him? You're more insane and delusional than I thought."

"Look around you," Harriet pointed to the men that were keeping her locked inside this building and who had hunted her down like a dog. "Do you think that my husband has the command of anyone of importance? You think that there is anyone out there that is going to listen to him who is important?

A bunch of old bureaucrats and a bunch of flower children dreaming of different days aren't going to stop the legion of followers that I have with me. In the end, the person who gets the final say is the one with the stronger army and I have the stronger army."

"You're a psychopath," Tara said bitterly. "Everyone knows it and everyone says it behind your back, but I'm not afraid to say it to your face."

"And you're a whore," Harriet growled back. "Don't pretend like I'm an idiot. I know that my husband is trying to get rid of me. He's been trying to get rid of me since the moment we were arranged to be married. I know that my husband is a progressive fool who thinks that he can change the world just because he has the idealistic notions that those of you on the bottom also deserve to be in the middle and on the top. No one will ever agree to this and it will lead to war.

I'm trying to save our pack and our people. The moment the other packs see that there is weakness among us, they will flood our borders and they will destroy all of us. Our strongest will abandon us and they will go to those who think that they can protect us better. Can't you see that? Those who matter will abandon us to those who are weak. Grayson will be the death of us all."

161

"You doubt that there is anyone in the lower ranks of the pack that would be worthy of standing and protecting the pack?" Tara asked her, thinking about Tina and Greg and Laura. She thought about the myriad of others who were great people too, but silenced by the oppression of people like Harriet who thought that status determined whether a person was strong or weak. It wasn't fair.

"I doubt that or they would be higher in the ranks," Harriet said bluntly. "But my husband is a fool who thinks that people like you should have a say in the matters of those who are better than them."

"Maybe I don't personally deserve that," Tara said, knowing that she wasn't the kind of person who deserved or wanted a position of power and authority, but she knew that people like Greg and Laura specifically would have been brilliant. Laura was cunning and wise at the same time. She saw things clearly and understood what was important when there were plenty of factors at play.

Greg was the kind of man who was dedicated and determined to master what was important. Both of them would have made brilliant leaders in the pack, but they were deprived of that because they were from other packs or born of lower ranking parents. That was the wrong reason to keep them below the decks.

"But I know many who are better than you are and would be more worthy of taking leadership than you and Grayson is right. He's been right all along that you elitist fools don't deserve to lead. Maybe that will drive away members of the pack, but we don't need them. It'll be refining, making us stronger. So you and all of your followers can go try to join some other pack or clan. You can feel what it's like to be second class citizens while you eat away at each other."

"Spoken like a true idealist." Harriet shook her head, feeling the words gnawing at her and she could feel the truth of it. Tara knew that this was the reason why she was so terrified of Tara and Grayson. She knew that the pack would rebel against her and that they would get rid of her. They wouldn't need her and that meant that they would take over the whole pack and outcast her.

There would be no one left to save her. There would be no one out there who would care about Harriet or the others. They would be destroyed by the very barbaric notions that they lived by in their archaic world. "No wonder Grayson loves you," Harriet sneered angrily. "I bet he thinks that you two are truly destined for each other. That the two of you are actually meant to be together, like the two of you are kindred spirits."

"Maybe that's why he doesn't love you and is trying to figure out how to destroy you," Tara proposed defiantly, tired of feeling like a victim. She wouldn't stand by anymore and she wouldn't let this woman tear at her. No. She was ready to fight back. No more running away, no more being afraid. She was the kind of woman who was ready for a fight and who was ready to give Harriet the kind of fight that she deserved.

"Love?" Harriet laughed. "You think far too highly of love. No one ever cares about love. Love is something that only poor people and the weak care about. Love doesn't keep you warm at night and it doesn't keep you fed. Love doesn't make the wheels of the world turn and it doesn't make sure that bad things don't happen to the good people of the world. Love is just a novel idea to make the weak think that they have a purpose for living. It's a lie that we all conveniently tell the inferior people to give them hope in all the wrong places."

"You're a sad, bitter woman," Tara said to her. "I'm going to be glad when you're done with and destroyed. I'm going to be the one who hopes that they banish you, rather than kill you. I hope that you have to go groveling to some pack for the lowest position just to be safe. It'll be a good day when I watch you get destroyed."

"And how exactly am I going to get destroyed?" Harriet laughed at that. "You realize that just by having you, I've already won this little battle between my husband and myself? You realize that even if you don't cooperate with me, I have everything I need just by keeping you in my possession. After all, you can lie all you want and you can try to fight me, but in the end, that baby in your belly is going to make sure that there is no hope for you or him."

"Doesn't matter," Tara said. "You can believe whatever you want."

Tara stood up from her chair and she could hear the men behind her shuffling and taking a step toward her. They were nervous and they were worried, even if Harriet wasn't. That was good, they would start to splinter and break against Harriet if they didn't trust her and they thought that there was actually something up Tara's sleeve that would be of importance. All she needed was for them to think that she had something strong against Harriet. If they didn't have their blind faith in her, then maybe they would be willing to make a deal.

"I didn't say you could leave," Harriet growled.

"Doesn't matter," Tara reached into her pocket and pulled out her cellphone, tossing it onto the desk. "Say hello to Grayson for me."

The biggest mistake that Harriet had made was to tell her men that Tara wasn't someone that they should be worried about. They saw her as a frightened little rabbit that was on the run, trying to hide from them. They saw her as weak and fearful, someone who wouldn't resist and someone who had no fight in them.

They thought that she was scared and when Harriet looked at the phone and saw that she was being recorded on Grayson's voicemail, there was a dread that didn't just linger inside of her. It spread out like a virus to the men that were in her employment. Tara could feel all the walls and all the munitions that Harriet thought she'd stored up exploding and bursting all around her. There was no safety net, there was no security, and there was nothing protecting them now.

"You should have told your men to search me," Tara said bluntly. "I guess that you probably should have known your enemy a little better."

"God damn you," Harriet grabbed a paperweight from Luke's desk and smashed the phone to pieces. It didn't matter. She could smash it all she wanted to, but the message had been running. Every time they came to a pause, Tara would hang up and call back. It took thirty seconds to hit the voicemail. There were at least four messages on Grayson's phone. She didn't even know, maybe Grayson had answered one of them and was recording it.

Either way, it was only a matter of time before Harriet and everyone else was discovered. Harriet glared at the men behind Tara. "Why didn't you search her?" Harriet shrieked at the top of her lungs. "Why didn't you take away her phone?"

"You said that she was on the run," the man behind her bumbled and blustered. "We didn't think that she would do anything smart like that."

"Thanks," Tara quipped. "Either way, you're running out of time. I suggest all of you start to consider whether you want to be on Harriet's side when this thing blows up or if you want to be on the victor's. Grayson is going to come down on you all with everyone else that didn't join you."

"Don't listen to her," Harriet snapped. "She's just trying to get inside of your head. Take her up to the VIP lounge and hold her there. If Grayson shows up, we're still going to have enough men to take care of him. Get her out of here now and I don't want anyone visiting her at all. One guard is to watch over her and that is it. No letting her talk to anyone else."

"Fine by me," Tara said. She knew the VIP lounge like the back of her hand and if she was going to have to wait somewhere for rescue, then she wouldn't prefer any other place.

"Fine, but we need to have a serious chat," the Hangover said with a stern voice that meant that he was the one who was probably at the most risk right now. Sure he was. They were all in serious trouble if Harriet didn't come up with a miracle soon. He grabbed Tara by the arm and pulled her up from her seat and they headed toward the door of the office. She glanced over her shoulder at Harriet who looked like she was about to vomit as she glared at the shattered remains of the phone in front of her.

Good.

She needed to be scared.

CHAPTER TEN

The VIP lounge was dim and it was the kind of silence that made her wonder if there was going to be any point to sitting up here. There was something brewing on the horizon and she knew that she was responsible for it, but she was terrified of it all the same. There was something dangerous at work and she could be the one who just set off everything horrible that was about to happen. What was she supposed to do if a war broke out and she was being held hostage up here? She figured that she would transform and try to kill the guard, but she hated to think about things like that.

Hangover had left her in the hands of someone else. He berated and shouted at her guard for what felt like an hour about how he wasn't to touch her, talk to her, or let anyone else come near her. The guard looked at his boss with the kind of stone cold expression that told Tara that he didn't know what was happening just yet. There was going to be some serious stuff going down very soon and she knew that he was going to be completely blindsided by everything that was revealed to him.

"If she tries to talk to you," Hangover said, shooting a glance at Tara, "don't listen to a thing she says. You watch her until I come and get you personally, or Harriet. No one else, you hear me?"

"I understand," the guard said. His eyes darted over to Tara who was sitting on the couch, taking off her coat and putting it beside her. She could feel his eyes traveling up and down her body, taking her in. She knew that he wanted her, just like most of the other men that she encountered in her life, but rather than repulse her, that made her excited.

There was hope that he was going to listen to the beautiful woman that he was in charge of watching over. She wanted him to be willing to listen. The more people who turned against Harriet, the better. She knew that there were more than four people already who were doubting her, and there couldn't be that many more out there that were deeply loyal to her. She was digging at the sores that were already there.

When Hangover left, Tara looked at her guard who stared across at the mezzanine. Tara wondered if he was even aware that there was a second exit to this place. She could very literally get up and walk out of here if he kept his back to her the entire time. She was stealthy and she was sneaky. That was something that she had always been very good at. Slipping out of sight was something that she excelled at. When you're being chased by hunters, you have to learn to be that way if you want to survive.

She stood up and yawned, drawing his attention as she walked toward the bar, getting him used to the sounds of her moving. She wanted him to do that. If he got used to sounds, then he wouldn't be alerted if she cautiously a run for it. He looked at her and she could feel his eyes lingering, drinking her in as he watched her. She didn't recognize him from the meeting on New Year's Eve. She wondered if he was someone new.

"Why don't you sit back down?" he said nervously, gesturing toward the couch.

"I'm thirsty," she said. "Do you want a drink? I'm not an amazing bartender, but I could make the basics with my eyes closed. I don't know; you're not the kind who looks like he's into cocktails. You look like you're a straight kind of guy."

"I prefer beer myself," he said with a shrug. That was good. He was willing to talk.

"So what do you think about all of this?" she asked him, reaching into the fridge and pulling out a craft beer. It would have cost someone eight bucks downstairs, up here, it was thirteen, but for this guy, he was getting it on the house.

"Don't know what you're talking about," he looked at the gorgeous woman holding a beer for him and she knew that this must have been his fantasy. What would he give to have a gorgeous woman at home holding a beer for him when he got off work? The more she could play to his fantasy, the more likely he would be to listen to her.

"They didn't tell you?" She raised an eyebrow, but she wasn't truly surprised at all. No doubt Hangover and Harriet were trying their hardest to contain the information that they were totally screwed.

"Tell me what?" The guard looked at her with a confused expression.

"I had my phone when Harriet confronted me," Tara grinned as she walked out from behind the bar and handed her guard the beer. He took it and she could tell that he was starting to put the pieces together. He knew that there was something fishy going on already and this was just confirming his suspicions.

"I called Grayson and he heard the entire thing. He's coming to get me with the entire pack behind him. Harriet, your boss, everyone is going to make sure that you all burn for this. I'm sure Harriet is already trying to figure out some kind of cushy deal for herself and your boss, but you lower level enforcers, you're going to get the axe, I'm sure of it."

He looked at her with horrified eyes, wide with terror and worry. Even if Grayson was the kind of bloodthirsty monster that Harriet was, she knew that he would never just kill off his wife's supporters. In fact, they would probably get the lighter sentence and Harriet would get the worst. But, he didn't know that. None of them knew that.

He took the beer from her and had a swig, his eyes full of confusion, the gears in his mind turning and starting to figure out just where he stood in all of this. If he was figuring out the part he was going to play, then the others were going to figure it out as well.

"He's coming for you?" the guard asked. "And he knows all about this?"

"Every last thing." She nodded in assurance.

"Listen, I was just following orders," the guard said nervously. "Paul gives me an order and I figure that I'm supposed to do what he says or he'll kill me or have me banished for something. I didn't know that she was trying to throw some kind of coup or nothing."

He gave too much away. He knew everything that he was doing, but Tara was savoring the fear and the terror that was welling up inside of him. She knew that he was terrified and that this fear was no doubt spreading through the faction that Harriet had created right under her husband's nose.

Everything was coming down on them. No matter how many of these lackeys she had, they were going to be outnumbered and civil war was going to ruin any plans she had of having the kind of power that the pack currently had. She had to know that this was coming to an end.

"You'll tell him that I've been good to you, right?" the man asked her with a horrified expression on his face that feared that she might do the opposite of vouch for him. "I let you get a drink and walk around and stuff. You'll tell him that right?"

"Maybe," she shrugged. "I'd suggest you go tell the others and maybe all of you should go have a chat with your boss. Don't worry about me. I'll be up here, waiting for Grayson to show up with his army of very angry and very pissed supporters. After all, it's not like I have anywhere to go right now."

"Listen, have whatever you want," he said nervously, taking a step toward the exit. "I'll have a chat with Paul and the others. Maybe we can get you out of here before this gets out of hand."

"I'm in no hurry," she said with a smile, sitting back down on the couch.

She watched him as he rushed out of the VIP lounge and across the walkway to the mezzanine where there was another guard posted. She could see them whispering and when they both looked over at her, glancing at her, she wiggled her fingers at them, waving hello. It wasn't long until the two of them were gone down the staircase to tell the others and to spread word that their doom was upon them. She liked that it had been so easy to dismantle them.

When they were gone however, she knew that Paul the Hangover wasn't going to stand for this and he was going to be pissed at her turning more of the guards against them. She stood up and grabbed her coat, heading for the curtained off room behind the bar where the guard clearly hadn't expected there to be a room. She slipped into the room and down the stairs quietly, looking into the kitchen to see if there was anyone posted in there to keep an eye out. Since it had an easy access out into the alleyway behind the club, she figured that there would be someone.

She was right. There was a guard sitting with his back to her. He was on the prep table, his legs dangling as he stared at the door leading to the alleyway, clearly not expecting anyone to come down the stairs. She watched him and waited for a moment. There had to be some way out of this. Quietly, she slipped down the stairs and hid behind one of the multitude of stations in the kitchen and waited for her chance to present itself.

There was a loud bang beyond the room and there were a series of louder bangs that followed. She realized that there was someone knocking on the front door and it drew the man on guard duty's attention just as quickly as it drew hers. He hopped down off the table and walked across the kitchen, almost spotting Tara as she lurked behind one of the tables, in the gloom if the kitchen that was barely hiding her at the moment. The man looked through the doorway and leaned against the doorframe, listening as the door opened.

"Grayson," Harriet's voice was distant, but it wasn't hard to hear. It was so quiet in the club that you could hear a pen drop. She shuffled out of her hiding spot and headed toward the island bank of burners and tables. The man at the doorway didn't even look her direction. He was engrossed with what was unfolding outside and truthfully, so was Tara. "What a pleasant surprise."

"Where is she?" Grayson demanded. "I received a series of phone calls from one of our discouraged and terrified members of our pack. I don't like what I heard from them, Harriet."

"You mean your mistress?" Harriet tried to clarify. "The one that you've been in league with to throw me out of my rightful position and to make us all equals."

"What are all of you doing here?" Grayson asked the guards that were standing around. "My power-hungry wife has clearly made you all wonder about her stability and her mental state. Are you going to stand around and expect her to reward you when all of this is over? What do you think you're going to get out of bullying and harassing a low member of our pack? My parents are already aware of what has happened here and they're furious. It's only a matter of time before they demand justice be done."

"Why would your parents worry about a worthless bottom member?" Harriet snapped. "He's lying or they would have been here already."

"Because our pack is built like a pyramid, Harriet," Grayson reminded her. Tara smiled at the sound of his voice. God, she loved it. It was the kind of voice that made her feel warm and happy inside. "If you upset the bottom and they realize that they're being treated like second-class citizens, they're going to rise up and they're going to destroy all of us, something that none of us are interested in."

"They are inferior," Harriet snapped. "They cannot harm us."

"Tell that to the hundreds of them that are already whispering about how you have kidnapped and tortured one of their own," Grayson said sternly.

"We haven't laid a finger on her," one of the guards barked with a hint of worry in his voice. There was desperation there and everyone could hear it. Harriet's ranks were crumbling beneath her and there was nothing that she could say or do that would save them now. Everything was falling apart and Tara couldn't help but smile. The man in the doorway had stopped leaning, clearly just now learning what was going on. He stood there nervously watching.

"That's not what they're saying beyond these walls," Grayson told them. "The low levels are rallying and they're demanding your head, Harriet and the heads of all those who helped you intimidate, kidnap, torture, and keep secret everything that has transpired here. The truth is essentially irrelevant right now, but if you give me the girl, I'm sure that I can vouch for the safety of your people, but they're going to want your blood either way, I'm sure."

"Don't listen to him," Harriet ordered her men. "He's trying to trick us and it isn't going to work. If there were any who were interested in stopping us or standing with him, they would have come with him. He's bluffing."

"What if he's not?" the familiar voice of the guard who had been watching her piped up. He was terrified and he had fallen completely under Tara's spell and she had scared him into realizing that there was a massive problem. "Think about it, what are we going to gain if Harriet is right? We'll just end up being in the same spot that we already are. If we turn her over to Grayson and his plot is hatched, at least some of us will have a chance to rise."

"All of you will," Grayson assured them. "My society would be built upon the belief that every man could rise upon the merits of his character and his skills. Each of you can be as valuable as you want to be. But right now, you need to make a decision as to where you stand in this fight. If you're with Harriet, then you're going to end up on the losing side and I can't protect you."

There was a shift of light in the kitchen and Tara turned to the source. It was the back door to the alleyway and she saw a figure in the shadows squeeze through the small gap of light before shutting the door very cautiously and very quietly. She turned and saw that the figure sneaking into the kitchen was very familiar. It was Greg.

He crept like a panther across the kitchen and sneaked up behind the guard, who had his back to Greg, watching what was happening outside with the others. He was terrified and he was completely absorbed in the events that were unfolding. Greg was as quiet as a shadow and when he stood behind the man, he was poised for the strike. It was as fast as lightning, like a viper lashing out.

His arms wrapped around the guard's neck and Tara watched as he applied pressure to all the right places and the guard's eyes fluttered before his whole body went limp, passing out and falling over. Greg guided him to the floor and when the guard came to rest, he looked up and saw Tara standing just feet away from him.

When Greg spotted her, he held a finger up to his lips and motioned for her to follow him. She suddenly realized that Harriet was right. There wasn't an army coming for them. In fact, this was all a massive bluff to get her out of here and nothing more. There was something inside of her that felt dismayed at the fact that everything she had worked for was falling apart because Grayson hadn't taken advantage of it.

They could have told Grayson's parents or other low level Shifters of what was happening, but the decided to do this weird rescue mission instead. She knew that she was going to blow up on them when she had the chance.

"Come on," Greg whispered to her, taking her by the arm and leading her to the doorway that led out into the alley. He gently pushed the door open and let her go out first where Tina was waiting in an outfit that

177

looked like she was ready to sneak in and kill the prime minister of some communist nation. She looked at Tina, who glanced up and down the alleyway to make sure that they were safe before she led the way.

"What about Grayson?" Tara asked as they ran as quickly as they could.

"How did you end up in the kitchen?" Greg ignored the question as they ran to safety. "Were they really holding you in the kitchen?"

"No," Tara shook her head. "I was convincing the guards that Grayson would bring an army with him when you guys came for me. They were all turning on Harriet and I slipped down from the VIP lounge to the kitchen. I just had to get rid of one more guard and I was free."

"Well," Greg shrugged nervously. "Plans have changed. Things aren't working out the way that we thought."

At the end of the alleyway, a fancy silver car came to a stop, cutting them off and she felt the familiar terror of being trapped creeping up inside of her stomach. She hated this feeling. She hated that they were always one step ahead of her. She froze and watched as Tina ran to the car and opened the passenger's door. She saw that Laura was behind the wheel and felt a wave of relief.

She was officially rescued.

***

"What about Grayson?" she asked again, feeling nervous and terrified that no one was answering her about him. Was he sacrificing himself for her while she got away? She didn't understand why he would do that trade, but the fact that he was coming to rescue her was enough to make her want to swoon and kiss him all over. He was the most heroic man that she knew and she was grateful for him.

"Grayson is going to be fine," Tina assured her, but there was something inside of her voice that worried her. "We just have to get you to the airport and everything is going to be just fine."

"Why are we going to the airport?" Tara didn't understand. They had Harriet. They had her by the throat and they could get rid of her once and for all. This wasn't something that they needed to do for the sake of romance, but rather for the sake of goodness to the people of their pack. They deserved to be free of the tyranny that she was promoting and that she was going to spread throughout their people. She was going to enslave them. She was going to make everything worse if they just let her get away with all of this. No, Tara couldn't accept this. They couldn't be running away.

"We're going to meet Grayson's parents at the airport," Greg told her. "Listen, things are not going the way that you might have wanted them. The higher ups in the pack are furious and the lower levels are demanding blood. Most of them don't know what's going to happen or what they want blood for, they just know that they're unhappy. It seems that both Grayson and Harriet are matched in trying to convert the entire pack to their cause. Now, it's blowing up all around us."

That didn't make sense to her. How could people still be siding with Harriet and how could they possibly think that there was any way that they were going to lose if Harriet was brought to trial? She practically got her laughing and cackling maniacally on the phone. That had to count for something huge. People couldn't just sit by and let that slip their minds. They needed to actually stand up for themselves.

"I don't understand how this can be happening," Tara shook her head and waited as Laura drove them through New York City, heading for the airport to have a meeting that was going to change the course of the pack and probably the world of all Shifters in New York City for the rest of their lives. There was going to be no hiding after this. There was no running away.

This was going to be the end of the life that every single one of them knew up to this point. If there was a civil war brewing, then she supposed that it was their responsibility and their duty to make sure that they averted it to the best of their ability. They needed to make sure that there was no blood shed for the right cause or even the wrong cause. People needed to know that there was something in between.

That was where Grayson excelled. He was a man who knew how to talk and he knew how to listen too. If there was anyone in the pack that was going to come to a positive conclusion or find a way to settle all of the accounts that felt like they were wronged, it was going to be him. He was going to make sure that everyone was happy and that everyone was satisfied before more insanity and more violence could be spread among the pack.

The weight of the situation started to come down on her as she looked out the window. She knew that there were more than just their own pack watching for the resolution of this crisis. There were a dozen packs, clans, tribes, or prides in New York City alone who were directly in contact with their pack who would be watching to see what transpired.

If the old traditions held, then they would follow suit. If the new way of progress and equality was allowed in, then maybe they would follow suit, maybe they would laugh and keep their old ways, or maybe they would see the pack as weak and strike out at them. Either way, things were going to change, and that was enough to make everyone nervous.

They pulled up to the airport and it was typically busy for the holiday season. Next week, they were going to have to deal with the arrival thousands of people coming back from their holiday vacations and returning to school. That meant that everything was jammed and packed, but they made their way into one of the parking garages and found a spot to park the car.

She didn't think to ask where they got the car, but she supposed that it didn't matter. It had served its purpose for them and they were finally at the airport. They were safe and they were going to get away scot free from all of this mess. Well, maybe not scot free, but at least they weren't in a position of weakness like they had been before. They were going to be able to negotiate now. They were going to be able to fight standing up.

"Grayson should be here shortly," Greg said, checking his phone. Clearly he was in communication with Grayson, which made Tara jealous that she wasn't the one who was talking to him. She wanted to be there with him and she wanted to be the one who was at his side.

She wanted to hear his voice and when they walked toward the airport, she knew that something grim was on the horizon. All she could do was pray that she would get a future that would be kind to her child. She couldn't care less about the suffering that she would endure. All she wanted was to make sure that their child would be fine.

Inside the airport, there was a conference room that had been reserved. The fact that there were conference rooms in the airport surprised Tara, but she figured that there were a lot of things in the world that she didn't know about. They walked through the busy, bustling building, avoiding people who looked unsavory and she could have sworn had knowledge in their eyes. They had looks that told her that some of these people were probably not as ignorant as they appeared. They probably knew exactly what was happening and they knew what a Shifter was and what a pack was.

Some of them, might even be able to turn into wolves when they needed to power to. That scared her more than anything else in this situation. If this place was crawling with Shifters and a war broke out, there would be no hiding it. There would be no stopping the populace at large of knowing it. That would mean mass panic and that would mean that there were hunters on the horizon.

These Shifters in New York City with their enormous packs of hundreds didn't know the terror of hunters and how relentless they were. They didn't know what it was to go to sleep wondering if you'd wake up in the middle of the night to a raid where they would kill you and all those that you loved.

They didn't know what their true enemy was. It wasn't each other. They had forgotten that. Tara had not and she never would. As she followed Greg and the others, she watched them walk toward a door that was flanked by two guards each. They looked like they belonged in the Secret Service the way they stood so ominously and intimidatingly.

"This is it," Tina said as they opened the doors and let Tara enter alone. "Good luck," she said to her friend with a soft, sweet smile on her face. She knew that Tara was in a dangerous position and she was scared for her friend. Tara hugged Tina and knew that she was very lucky to have such people in her life with her.

Inside the room, she realized that she was not alone. She watched as the figure turned and she saw that it was Grayson. She ran to him the moment the door closed and she threw her arms around him, embracing him and hugging him with all of her strength. She never thought that she would be so excited and so eager to hug a man.

She hugged him and she knew that she would never get over him. She knew that this was the one man that she was destined to be with, even if that road ended here. She wanted him to know that. She wanted him to be aware of how much she loved him and how much she wanted him to be in her presence.

"I've missed you," she breathed into his neck.

"I missed you too," he told her honestly. "Listen," he said, pulling back from her. "I know that things are terrifying, but I need you to trust me. I'm going to do whatever is necessary for us. I'm going to make sure that we're safe, because that's all that I care about right now. All I care about is that we get out of this together. I don't care what happens beyond that."

"They said that Harriet has an army and that there's talk of civil war," Tara breathed, horrified about what the implications might be. "Are you ready for that? What can we do to stop that? How can we stop her from attacking innocent people?"

"I will do whatever I need to," he said honestly and she was scared of what that might mean. He leaned in and kissed her, trying his hardest to take the fear away from her, but she knew that there was nothing that could take this fear away from her.

This was dread. This was the kind of thing that made her want to pass out from all of the horrors that were around her. "I love you, Tara," he said honestly to her. She knew that the genuine truth in his voice was more than she could have ever wanted to hear. He was all that she needed and she reminded herself of that. She just needed to follow his lead and everything was going to be okay. Grayson was going to make sure that everyone walked away with something that they wanted. That was all that mattered to him in the end. He was a diplomat and this was his time to shine.

"What do you need me to do?" Tara asked him.

"Don't be afraid of the truth," he told her honestly. "Just say what you must when they ask you. If they want to know the truth about something, tell them. I'm not ashamed of what I've done and I know that you are the woman that I truly love. I'm not giving up on us and I never will."

She swallowed hard and thought about the implications of that. She wasn't sure that she could do it. She wasn't sure that she could sit down and tell the truth about what happened. Could she genuinely tell his parents that they had been having an affair and that she was carrying their grandchild?

It was too late to decide.

The doors opened.

THE FINAL CHAPTER

There was a sort of regality that swirled around his parents. They were both the results of impeccable breeding that had been happening from clans for ages now. Their marriage was one of political importance, just like Grayson's marriage to Harriet had been. Luckily for them, their marriage had worked and now Grayson's was on the brink of causing civil war between the entire pack. That was something that they were going to have to address and she knew that they were going to be horrified by it.

His mother had long dark hair and bright hazel eyes that looked exactly like her son's. She was a woman with sharp, harsh features that showed no love and no mercy toward her son or for the woman that he was accused of having an affair with. It was clear to Tara that she was not happy with what her son had done and she was here to make sure that justice was done to her son and the woman who had caused so much trouble.

As she walked toward the chair that her husband pulled out for her, Tara was certain that Grayson's mother was sitting in a position where she was in favor of Harriet. She understood what it was like to be a victim of the process of arranged marriage and the significance of it. Harriet was going to have her support and that worried Tara. How was she going to sway this cold woman to her side?

186

Grayson's father didn't look any happier. He was older and his hair was gray from the time that he had spent on this earth and she was certain that his office had probably caused him to gray as well. How many times had he been threatened with civil war? How many times had he been forced to quell these kinds of situations?

His eyes were bright blue and they were distant, like he was tired of all of this and ready to relinquish his power to his son, but this was bringing the stability of his retirement into question. Could he relinquish the post when his son had brought the pack to civil war with his reckless actions?

Tara was beginning to feel guilty for the pain and the suffering that her actions had caused his family. She didn't want them to hurt or to feel badly about themselves. She didn't want them to be in the kind of agony that she was certain she'd brought for them. This was her doing and as his father sat down, she knew that Grayson was going to try and take as much of the blame as possible. She would not let him fall on his sword alone.

"Let us cut to the chase of the matter," Grayson's father said with a deep voice that was filled with the authority and power that they had expected him to have. He was clearly a strong man who had used that voice to tear down many enemies in the past. His father was a warrior, a man who was unlike any other who had lived before them in the pack.

It was by his father's hands that brought New York to its knees and the warring Shifter gangs were brought under one banner or destroyed completely. There was no middle ground with him and there was no freedom for those who defied him. "Are the rumors true?"

"Yes," Tara jumped in before Grayson could say something that got himself in more trouble. She didn't want him protecting her. She wanted him to be by her side and she wanted him to be with her when all of this came crashing down. She didn't want to be alone with their child. "I am pregnant with the son of Grayson and I did so without coercion or ill intent. I love your son and I gave into my emotions when I saw the opportunity. The fault and the blame is mine."

"And I suppose my son tripped and fell on you over and over again," Grayson's mother said with a cold, pointed voice that stung with each word that escaped it. Her cold and merciless eyes gazed over at her son who was not taking this sitting down. He looked back at his mother and stared at her for a moment before she continued to goad him and lay into him. "I believed that I attended the marriage of my son some time ago. I had thought that he was already married at this point in his life. Perhaps I was mistaken in believing so. I certainly do not remember him marrying himself to this young upstart that just recently joined our pack."

"That was a marriage brought on by the whims of those above me," Grayson said grimly. "I do not hold for the archaic traditions and I am a staunch progressive. You know that I would not touch that woman if I was given all the money and all the power in the world. She is a viper and she is a monster that should be put down. I have the evidence I need to convict her of plotting a rebellion against me."

"It appears that you have created the rebellion yourself," his father shot at him with a cold voice. "The entire pack is rising up and demanding that there is war. A thousand factions are returning from old gangs and old rivalries. People are begging for a reason to have at each other and the two of you have given them sufficient reason to do so. Do you not realize that your actions have greater consequences than your own life?"

"Harriet is on her way to the meeting," Grayson told them. "I have confessed to my doing and I have expressed that I have no interest in hiding it. I am not afraid of that woman and I am more than willing to come to terms with her. However, should she have an intent to push for war, I will have no choice but to act rashly when she brings this to your attention."

"What makes you think that we will side with your rash decisions?" Grayson's mother asked him. Yes, it was clear now that she was definitely standing against her son and that she had no intent of fighting for him or for the cause that he had brought up.

They had to know of Grayson's progressive nature and that he hated the traditions of the Shifters. How could this be a surprise to them that he was going to dissolve the old way? "You would destroy the work and the ways of thousands who had come before you. I am a product of the traditions and so is your father. These are the tenants, the foundations of our people. You are spitting in everything that it means to be a Shifter."

"Am I?" Grayson barked. "How many sit on the pack's council who have done nothing for the pack or the world in general? How many of them are epicurean fools that take and take, but give nothing and do nothing for our people? The lower ranks are those that give back to us, who fight for us, and who supply us with everything that we need. Turning us into equals will do nothing but make us more effective and make us more powerful."

"It will tear us apart," Grayson's father declared angrily. "The higher ranks will leave us and our enemies will exploit their and turn against us to attack us when we are down. You do not know war, Grayson. You are weak and soft, but I suppose that this is all my doing. I am the one who kept you away from the ways that had molded and shaped me into the man that I am. I gave you a world of peace when you needed a world of war to make you into the kind of leader that we needed. Now, you've become an adulterous dreamer who has lost his way. No, I fear that all of this is ruined."

"I am your heir apparent," Grayson snapped at them angrily. "I have been making alliances of my own and I have an army of supporters behind me. If you throw your lot in with Harriet, I will have no choice but to go to war with her and with you two. I cannot allow you to enslave our people anymore because they were unfortunate enough not to be born into our pack."

Tara reached out and touched his arm. It was fine and inspiring when it was just words flying across the table at enemies. In real life, she knew that there was nothing further from the truth than that. War was a horrible thing and it was terrible. She wouldn't be the excuse that these two had to rip at each other and kill one another. She couldn't be that person and she wouldn't be able to live with herself. No, she needed him to stand down and she needed him to realize that this was madness.

Grayson turned and looked at her. She could see the fear and the terror in his eyes that he wasn't going to succeed. She could tell that he was afraid that they were going to have to go to war and that everything was going to fall apart. War would weaken them and old enemies would come for them and old allies would turn and betray them.

Things would only get worse from that moment on and they all feared why and how that might happen. She shook her head, but she knew that things were in his hands. She couldn't make these decisions for him. After all, he was the heir apparent of the pack and he was the future Alpha. Most already recognized him as the Alpha. In the end, this was his decision.

Across the room, the door to the conference room opened and Harriet stalked into the room. She was as radiant and as beautiful as a statue, walking with the poise and the presence that made Tara feel like she was slouching. She was the kind of angel of vengeance and death that made everyone fearful. As she walked, her eyes were locked on Grayson who was meeting her gaze with the same hatred and the same defiance as he was receiving from her.

They were impossible, like two children who hated each other. Tara felt out of place here. This was not a conversation that she needed to be a part of. This was something beyond her. She hadn't even been allowed to attend the pack meetings or the council meetings.

"Hello husband," Harriet growled, sitting down at the table and looking at him with such venom and hatred that it was palpable. It felt like they were all drowning in it. Everyone was seated at equal points around the table so that there were no clear lines, no clear alliances that had been made.

Tara knew that whoever was going to receive the support of Grayson's parents was going to walk out of this room the victor. Even if the other declared war, the loser was not going to have the numbers to win the war. They were not going to have the support that they wanted or that they needed to take over the pack. It would be brief and bloody. Tara felt like she was the prize here. They were fighting over her presence, after all. They were fighting because she was there right then and that was all they wanted to settle. Why was Tara here? How were they going to right the wrong that her presence made.

"Do not call me that, monster," Grayson snarled at her.

"Very well," Harriet said to him, smiling playfully as she looked across the table at Grayson's parents. "You know what I'm demanding. I want him deposed and I want everything that he has. You know that I am your spiritual successor and that I see you as a father just as much as my own." Harriet looked at Grayson's mother with the kind of dark and wicked eyes that made Tara's stomach feel nauseous.

They were mirrored in the cold, distant face of Grayson's mother, who met Harriet's piercing gaze. "I have always seen you as more of a mother to me, even more than my own mother who was weak compared to you. I would make the two of you proud and I would make sure that the pack endures and survives to see a new day, a day more glorious than any of us could have ever imagined. But, I cannot do that while your son exists.

"As you both know, Grayson has been making himself the champion of the people who are lesser than us. He thinks that pups should lead the pack and that our elders and our betters are weaker than they really are. He needs a lesson in the superiority of the higher levels, because he has gotten soft and does not know what true war is. He's brought the weaker levels to the brink of war and they're calling for blood.

You can see what it is that he's done to the order and the stability of our pack. If you let him take control of the pack, he is going to destroy everything that both of you have fought for. Everything that our ancestors and our elders have bled and suffered for will turn to ashes in his touch.

You need someone strong who understands what it was that was happening when you declared war on the other packs and you brought the wolves together. We're no longer wandering nomads and gangs that fight over city blocks. We're an empire now and I will see to it that we endure as an empire. Even yesterday, he compromised with the bears. I fear that going forward, he is going to ruin everything if you do not stop him now."

"And what would you have us do to our own son?" Grayson's father asked her with a voice that was thunderous and booming with power. "This is my own flesh and blood and you are asking that I take his inheritance away, everything that I have worked to give him. After all, the matters that I have entrusted him with have all been successes. He has proved himself to be a leader of great renown and of great skill. He has negotiated with enemies and brought us victories."

"Victories that are tiny compared to what you could have done," Harriet laughed at the sound of that. "Victories that could have been so much greater had I been the one entrusted with the task. You know that he is weak and that he is trying his hardest to make peace with those that are his lesser. I want you to give me his inheritance and entrust me with the keeping of your empire. I want him banished from these lands and I want him to be sent away under the threat of death should he ever return."

"You would have us banish our own child?" Grayson's mother said the words, but there was no actual concern in her voice. There was no horror or panic at the thought that her own son might be sent away. No, this was just her repeating the words that ran across her mind of things that she should say. Tara was horrified at a woman who could be so callous to her own son. She never wanted to be the kind of mother that this woman was attempting to be.

"I would," Harriet answered with a smirk on her lips, like this was exactly what she wanted. "I would have his most powerful supporters put to death and I would have his whore executed for a symbol of our power and our severity of how much we hate those that would destroy what we have worked for. I would have her be a lesson to all of those who think that they can rise up against us."

"That is a lot of bloodshed," Grayson's father said as if this was something that was off putting to him. She looked at him and wondered if he wouldn't relish a taste of the old days where wolves tore out the throats of other wolves. "But, this is just one request. My son, what would you have?"

Tara touched Grayson's arm and they locked eyes for a moment. She didn't want bloodshed. She didn't want to be the reason that Grayson turned into the monster that he hated and that he committed the crimes and the sins that he abhorred his father of committing. No, she wouldn't be able to live with herself if she became the standard of blood that the rest of his life rallied behind. Not only would it destroy his soul, but it would kill her own soul as well.

"I would have Harriet divorced from me," Grayson said to them with a stern voice. "I would have her stripped of her title within the pack and then I would have her sent away. She would be banished from our lands under the threat of death and that is all.

I would not have her supporters killed and I would not have any more bloodshed. Her violent and archaic notions are no longer required of our people and I know that our people will see that and they will understand that the moment they are given the opportunity to think and see for themselves that they are more than just animals.

"However, I am not here looking for your support. I am here to come to terms with a traitor within our midst who thought that she could blackmail and threaten her husband into giving up the keys to the kingdom. I am not on trial here and I do not need to worry about what will happen to me. I am a man who is in need of only his own words and his own support. Her accusations toward me are true, but they do not merit a response.

"I am a progressive thinker and though she talks of empires and she talks of war and bloodshed, I am not of the same mind. We have forged an empire and we have crushed anyone who could even remotely stand up to us. We have no more equals and we have no more threats. We are beyond the touch of the nearest pack that is of any concern or danger. Now is a time for adaptation and growth that we can survive and that we can make ourselves into something new that our future generations can recognize and that they can be a part of."

"That is a radical notion," his father said with his head shaking. "It is also a folly that will destroy everything that I have worked for. There is no way that the empire can be maintained on the beliefs that we can simply change the order and we'll survive. Lower ranks may rise based on the merits of their duties and their services to the pack."

"But without war, there is no way for them to prove themselves and there are no more wars," Grayson declared. "Soon, you will be fighting the inside threat, those who are stuck in their lower levels and don't want to be there anymore. You will be fighting yourself and we will cannibalize ourselves if we are not careful. No, we need to change now before we start turning on one another.

Look at us right now! Look how eager we are to kill each other and to tear out each other's throats. If you send me away, the thought will linger and it will fester. It's too late for that and civil war will come back. If you kill my followers, then you will cement that in the minds of the neutrals and the people with undecided minds. They'll know that my people are right. There is no avoiding the inevitable. It will happen."

"So what are you suggesting then?" His father laughed. "Are you saying that we should side with you because of an inevitable revolution that might happen years down the road? Decades even?"

"No," Grayson said, turning and looking at Harriet. "I offer a middle ground that you're going to have to take if you want there to be peace."

"I don't have to accept anything," Harriet told him coldly. "I can decide for myself what I will or will not accept from you."

"Do whatever you wish," Grayson snapped at her. "But I am taking those who believe in me and my cause and we are leaving. Rather than kill one another, we will peacefully separate. I will sign a treaty so that there can be no war between the two packs and that we will not fight one another. I will make sure that there is nothing that we have to fear from each other.

But, I will demand that anyone who wishes to join my new society, that they be given the freedom and the passage to join me. We will start our own community and we will make sure that we are no bother to you or to the other members of the pack. It will be a fresh start for both factions."

"You think you can just rip the pack in half?" Harriet laughed. "I will never agree to this. If I agree to this, I will be seen as weak and I cannot have my own people questioning whether or not I can care for them and I can defend them. Anyone who attempts to leave with you, they will be hunted down and they will be killed."

"No they will not," Grayson's father said, standing up and holding up his hands. He looked around the room at all the faces that were present. Tara could feel the nerves in her stomach electrifying, burning a hole into her lining. It felt like her whole body had become an ulcer and that she was going to pass out.

She wanted that so badly. She wanted to have a life with Grayson where they were free of all of this and that they didn't have to worry about anything like war or death. She didn't want to have to look over her shoulder every time they were on the move. If there could be peace between the two packs and the two ideals, then they were in the right mind to take it.

They had to take care of each other and make sure that everyone was safe and protected. Their people needed to have a chance to forge the life that they wanted and that they deserved. This wasn't just a beautiful option, it was the only option that they had for themselves. This was their only chance at the life and the hope that they wanted.

"I have made my decision," Grayson's father said finally with a resolute sound in his voice that made Tara want to scream with the suspense. "Harriet, you will receive a divorce from my son due to his infidelity to you and for idealistic conflicts with the pack's code of standing. For this, you will receive the title, the position of inheritance, and the authority that was given to my son.

However, my son and his followers will be sent into binding exile to him. They will have to exist as an exiled band under threat of war. However, should they follow my son's lead, they will be given a peace treaty of protection. They will be given safe passage and transference to my son's new lands and they will be given the financial boon that was given to him in our inheritance. The two packs are to be allies and to never declare war upon each other. However, Harriet, should you break this code, then I will see to it that all of our allies and our enemies strike down you and your followers."

"This isn't fair," Harriet snapped. "You will be halving us."

"I suspect we will be doing more than that," Grayson's mother said finally. "The idea of equality is going to pull the majority of the lower levels and many of his supporters among the higher ranks. I would suggest that you start finding ways of placating and burying the hatchet between you and your ex-husband before your enemies start to circle. Perhaps he will make you into a protectorate pack."

"You can't do this!" Harriet shrieked.

"Perhaps you should show some gratitude," Grayson's father said with a smile on his lips. "After all, my son is right. Today is a new day and the days of war are behind us. If you would like to be the last cry of a dying generation, then so be it, but I would suggest you endure and find a way to salvage your lost kingdom."

***

Harriet did not heed their warning or take their advice. In fact, it wasn't long after the mass exodus to the Bahamas that word reached them that Harriet was already fighting a civil war within her pack for the throne that she had inherited. With less than fifty members remaining, those elitists who stuck with her thought that she was weak, that she had lost the majority of their empire to the whims of some idealistic boy.

When they whispered that she couldn't even keep a husband, so how was she supposed to keep an empire, her credibility went down in flames. The only way she was hanging on to her throne was by throwing them into war with a neighboring pack and giving them a common enemy.

The re-ignited gang wars between Shifters in New York City had the effect that Tara had seen coming all along. She knew that the war behind them was going to draw the scent of the hunters and it certainly did. Now, there were Shifters sneaking down to the Bahamas in groups of twos and threes, trying to submit themselves to the kindness of Grayson and his growing legions.

On the islands, they lived peacefully and they lived happily. They found jobs on the islands where they worked and played and grew with the kind of peace that Grayson had promised all of them. The fact that they were all equals now was enough to give them a lasting peace and democracy came to them. Some of them spread their wings and left the pack, going back to New York City to try and set up offshoots of the pack's ideology, and others went west to see if they could have luck elsewhere too. They were all considered friends and they were all given a promise of peace and protection from Grayson and the pack. There would never be a reason for them to ever fight one another. But they would always protect one another when they needed to.

In the Bahamas, they opened their own club for tourists and it quickly became the hottest attraction that the beach had to offer. In fact, the whole island was becoming envious of the tourists who had showed up out of nowhere and were making the island into the best destination in the Bahamas. It seemed like a natural thing to do. They all knew what it was like and they all knew their jobs down to a T. Besides, nothing was better than working with your best friends.

Greg and Tina finally found out that they truly were made for each other and they did end up finally tying the knot, just a few weeks after Grayson and Tara proclaimed their love to the world and married one another on the beach before the surf and the sky.

She had never been happier than her wedding day and even Laura found herself in love with a former high ranking member of the pack who was now on the council. Tara was certain that the two of them were going to become completely obsessed with one another and it wouldn't be long before they were married on the beach as well.

When little Natalie was born, it was the most joyous day of Tara's life and she knew that there would never be anything in her life that would come close to being a mother. When she held her daughter in her arms for the first time, it was like something clicked and she was given over to the kind of purpose and longing that she had been hoping for in her life.

She had everything that she needed. She had a child that made her life feel complete and a husband who loved her more than the world itself. She loved him as much as she possibly could and sometimes it felt like she was going to burst and explode from all the love in her life. It was overwhelming and it was a powerful love that made her sigh and stare off at the beach in euphoria.

Of course, when the nights came and Natalie was put down for the night, sleeping softly and pleasantly, completely unaware of the troubles her conception had caused, Tara would go back to her room and she would find her husband waiting for her. She would find him in bed, eager for her and she would find herself never getting used to the familiar hunger that was inside of her. After all, there was no getting over him and his talents and when she would scream in the middle of the night, it wasn't from nightmares.

THE END

Message From The Author:

Thanks so much for reading all the way to the end, I really hope you enjoyed it. If you did then you can check out and see ALL my other shifter releases by taking a look at __my Amazon page here!__

Also, if you could leave a rating that would be so helpful. Thanks in advance!

*

Get Yourself a FREE Bestselling Paranormal Romance Book!

Join the "**Simply Shifters**" Mailing list today and gain access to an exclusive **FREE** classic Paranormal Shifter Romance book by one of our bestselling authors along with many others more to come. You will also be kept up to date on the best book deals in the future on the hottest new Paranormal Romances. We are the HOME of Paranormal Romance after all!

* Get FREE Shifter Romance Books For Your Kindle & Other Cool giveaways

* Discover Exclusive Deals & Discounts Before Anyone Else!

* Be The FIRST To Know about Hot New Releases From Your Favorite Authors

Click The Link Below To Access Get All This Now!

SimplyShifters.com

Already subscribed?
OK, *Turn The Page!*

ALSO BY SIMPLY SHIFTERS....

SIMPLY ALPHA WOLVES
A TEN BOOK WEREWOLF ROMANCE COLLECTION

This unique 10 book package features some of the best selling authors from the world of Paranormal Romance. Well known names such as Amira Rain, Jasmine White, Ellie Valentina and more have collaborated to bring you a **HUGE** dose of sexy Alpha goodness. There will be love, romance, action and adventure alongside some hot mating in each of these 10 amazing books.

1 The Alphas Unwanted Mate – Ellie Valentina
2 The Alpha's Surrogate – Angela Foxxe
3 Legend Of The Highland Wolves– Bonnie Burrows
4 The Next Alpha – Jasmine White
5 Chained To The Alpha – JJ Jones
6 The Alphas Mail Order Mate – Jade White

7 The Wolf's Forbidden Baby – Ellie
Valentina
8 The Real Italian Alphas – Bonnie Burrows
9 Fated To The Alpha – Jasmine White
10 The Island Of Alphas – Amira Rain

START READING NOW AT THE BELOW LINK!

Amazon.com >
http://www.amazon.com/gp/product/B0167CVA26

Amazon UK >
http://www.amazon.co.uk/gp/product/B0167CVA2
6

Amazon Australia >
http://www.amazon.com.au/gp/product/B0167CV
A26

Amazon Canada >
http://www.amazon.ca/gp/product/B0167CVA26

Made in the USA
Coppell, TX
25 February 2023

13377228R00115